skins

contemporary Indigenous writing

Compiled by
Kateri Akiwenzie-Damm
and Josie Douglas

jukurrpa books

Kegedonce Press
Cape Croker Reserve
R. R. 5 Wiarton,
Ontario   N0H 2T0
Canada

IAD Press / Jukurrpa Books
PO Box 2531
Alice Springs
NT   0871
Australia

Jukurrpa Books is an imprint of IAD Press

National Library of Australia Cataloguing-in-Publication data

Skins : contemporary indigenous writing.

ISBN 1 86465 032 X.

1. Short stories, Australian - Aboriginal authors. 2. Short stories, New Zealand - Maori authors. 3. Short stories, Canadian - Indian authors. 4. Short stories, American - Indian authors. 5. Australian fiction - 20th century. 6. New Zealand fiction - 20th century. 7. Canadian fiction - 20th century. 8. American fiction - 20th century. I. Akiwenzie-Damm, Kateri, 1965- . II. Douglas, Josie, 1970- .

823.01088

Canadian Cataloguing-in-Publication data

Skins : contemporary indigenous writing

ISBN 0-9697120-6-5 (Kegedonce Press).—
      ISBN 1-86465-032-X (Jukurrpa Books)

1. Short stories, Australian—Australian aboriginal authors. 2. Short stories, New Zealand—Maori authors. 3. Short stories, Canadian (English)—Indian authors. 4. Short stories, American—Indian authors. 5. Australian fiction—20th century. 6. New Zealand fiction—20th century. 7. Canadian fiction (English)—20th century. 8. American fiction—20th century. I. Akiwenzie-Damm, Kateri, 1965- II. Douglas, Josie, 1970-

PR1309.S5S64 2000   823'.01088   C00-901212-5

Design by Louise Wellington, Jukurrpa Books
Printed in Australia by McPhersons Printers, Melbourne

Kegedonce Press gratefully acknowledges the support of the Canada Council for the Arts and DammWrite! Consulting and Communications.

The Canada Council for the Arts
Le Conseil des Arts du Canada

We acknowledge the support of the Canada Council for the Arts which last year invested $17.6 million in writing and publishing throughout Canada.

Nous remercions de son soutien le Conseil des Arts du Canada, qui a investi 17,6 millions de dollars l'an dernier dans les lettres et l'édition à travers le Canada.   *June 2000*

Acknowledgements

Maria Campbell   *Dah Teef*, from *Stories of The Road Allowance People*, by permission of the author

Thomas King   *Borders*, from *One Good Story, That One*, by permission of the author

Alootook Ipellie   *Love Triangle*, from *Arctic Dreams and Nightmares*, by permission of the author

Richard Van Camp   *Mermaids*, by permission of the author

Joseph Bruchac   *The Hungry One*, by permission of the author

Louise Erdrich   *Grandpa Kapshaw's Ghost*, from *Love Medicine*, by permission of the author

Linda Hogan   *Dora-Rouge's bones*, from *Solar Storms*, by permission of the author

Kimberly Blaeser   *Fancy Dog Contest*, from *Stories Migrating Home*, by permission of the author

Sherman Alexie   *The Farm*, from *The Raven Chronicles*, Fall 1996, by permission of the author

Patricia Grace   *It Used to Be Green Once*, from *The Dream Sleepers and Other Stories*, by permission of the author. *Ngati Kangaru*, from *The Sky People and Other Stories*, by permission of the author

Witi Ihimaera   *Life As It Really Is*, by permission of the author

Zion A. Komene   *Wairua is designed to flow in a Koru style*, by permission of the author

Briar Grace-Smith   *Charlie the Dreaded*, by permission of the author

Kenny Laughton   *Night Games* by permission of the author

Alexis Wright   *The Serpent's Covenant* by permission of the author

Melissa Lucashenko   *let me tell you what I want* by permission of the author

Bruce Pascoe   *Tired Sailor*, from *Shark*, by permission of Magabala Books and the author

Richard Frankland   *Who Took the Children Away?* by permission of the author

Sally Morgan   *The Letter* by permission of the author

Thanks

Chi Meegwetch

Izhi-zauginaun; mino-audjinaun to my friend and co-editor Josie Douglas. Together we came up with the idea for this anthology during a very long bus ride from Alice Springs to an Aboriginal community we visited in 1997. Many thanks to Marg Bowman, Brenda Thornley, Simon MacDonald and everyone at Jukurrpa and IAD Press. Mashkow-aendun! Special thanks to my family and friends, to the authors who have so generously shared their words and creativity, and to my assistant and friend Renée Abram for her invaluable work with Kegedonce. K'odaessinin.

To the Canada Council for the Arts for supporting this project, and the ongoing work of Kegedonce Press, I offer my sincere thanks. I especially would like to thank Paul Seesequasis for his work at the Canada Council. Finally, as always, ae-izhi-zauginaun to the ancestors, my community at Neyaashiinigmiing, my Elders and teachers, the land that sustains us, and the Creator who gives us all.

N'd'nawaendaugunuk
Kateri

I would like to thank all of the writers featured in this collection of short stories for agreeing to be part of this anthology, especially the Australian authors, whom I had the most to do with and from whom I learnt so much during the course of working on *skins*. Alexis Wright, Sally Morgan, Melissa Lucashenko, Kenny Laughton, Richard Frankland and Bruce Pascoe not only gave their talent, but their enthusiasm and good humour to this project. Thanks must also go to the staff at IAD Press for their dedication to this anthology: Brenda Thornley, Mandy Brett, Louise Wellington and Marg Bowman. Kateri Akiwenzie-Damm is the only person I know who doesn't sleep! This project could not have been realised without Kateri's joint involvement and it goes to show that bus rides on rough corrugated roads — while dusty and hot — can be very stimulating! A huge thank you to Kateri and Renée Abram at Kegedonce Press for their commitment and perseverance across the international timeline in seeing this project completed.

Josie

skins
contemporary Indigenous writing

Preface

We Remain, Forever

skins, contemporary Indigenous writing features the work of Indigenous writers and artists from many diverse First Nations in territories now known as Canada, the United States, Aotearoa (which the colonizers renamed New Zealand) and Australia. Some of these writers are well known internationally both within and beyond the Indigenous arts community. Others, though not as widely known, have made a big impact, winning awards and public acclaim for their work.

The work in this anthology is multi-dimensional, and from a wide array of styles, and cultural, linguistic, and artistic traditions. The writers come from diverse cultures and histories, from the far north of Canada to the south Pacific islands of Aotearoa. Despite these differences, what all of the writers share is our connection to our homelands, our histories of colonization, genocide, and displacement, and our will to survive and pass the treasures of our cultures to future generations. Most of us believe our creative work has a function well beyond self-expression. It expresses the values and aesthetics of our people and connects us to them and to our ancestors and future generations. It is a form of activism that both maintains and affirms who we are and protests against colonization and assimilation. It is a form of sharing, of giving back, of reaffirming kinship, of connecting with the sacredness of creation.

Some of you, many of you, may not have experienced before the beauty, complexity, humour, and diversity of Indigenous arts. For the most part, there is a form of what Paula Gunn Allen terms "intellectual apartheid" as well as what I would call "aesthetic apartheid" operating around the world. Our creative work, and there is a lot of it, going back thousands and thousands of years and forward to this day, continues to be segregated, denied, oppressed, ignored, silenced. And yet, it is essential to our communities and will never disappear, just as we remain, forever part of the land upon which the creator placed us.

All of us must feel the burden of history. We all must feel the need to restore our own art, to rehabilitate our art, to reconstruct our art, to reaffirm our art, to re-establish our own arts and culture. To create opportunities for all those people

who are heirs to those traditions to define for themselves, to define for ourselves,
for me to define for myself what I wish to happen, what you wish to happen, what
we all wish to happen for the people.

Witi Ihimaera, To See Proudly First Peoples Arts Conference, 1998

In collecting the work of Indigenous writers from Canada, the US, Australia and Aotearoa, Josie and I hoped to give readers a tantalizing taste of what is available, not only so that you would find this collection fulfilling but also to whet your appetite for more. In gathering the work of writers from Canada, the US and Aotearoa, I wanted to expose readers to the very best of our writers from those who have been groundbreakers in establishing our literary traditions to those who have proven to be among the brightest and most promising in recent years.

I am honoured to have been able to include the work of writers like Maria Campbell, Patricia Grace, Sally Morgan and Alootook Ipellie in this collection. Metis storyteller Maria Campbell is one of the most respected Native writers in Canada. Her groundbreaking, bestselling book *Halfbreed* is a classic in Canadian literature and has inspired generations of writers since it was first published in 1973. Patricia Grace's first collection of stories, *Waiariki*, published in 1975, was the first collection of stories by a Maori woman writer. Patricia continues to inspire Maori and other Indigenous writers around the world through her writing and her ongoing dedication in supporting the development of Maori and Indigenous writing and publishing. Sally Morgan's bestseller *My Place* is a part of the canon of Aboriginal literature in Australia and a must-read for any student of Indigenous literature. Inuit writer and visual artist Alootook Ipellie has been breaking trail for other Inuit and Arctic writers for more than twenty years. His collection of stories *Arctic Dreams and Nightmares* was the first collection of stories by an Inuk writer published in Canada. It was released in 1993.

It is also a great pleasure to be able to introduce you to some of our best, most accomplished "emerging" Indigenous writers. Among these writers are Richard Van Camp, Kim Blaeser, Richard Frankland and Briar Grace-Smith. Briar is an award winning playwright whose highly acclaimed play *Purapurawhetu* has been called "a new classic" in New Zealand drama and has toured nationally and internationally since its debut in 1997. Richard Frankland is an award winning writer and director of short films. Kim Blaeser, an Anishnaabe writer from Minnesota, is an Associate Professor of English at the University of Wisconsin-Milwaukee and a past winner of a First Book Award from the Native Writers' Circle of the Americas. Richard Van Camp has published a novel and two children's books and in 1997 won the Canadian Authors Association Air Canada Award as a young writer of "outstanding promise."

Some of the writing in *skins*, like Sherman Alexie's "The Farm" is clearly political. Some is not so obviously so. Yet, all of the stories seek to express certain truths about our realities as Indigenous peoples. Some, like Patricia Grace's "Ngati Kangaru", expose the lies in histories about us while others such as Richard Frankland's "Who Took The Children Away?" and Sally Morgan's "The Letter" look at the hidden tragedies and little known facts of historical and ongoing oppression. Thomas King's "Borders" takes on the sometimes inane laws and rules Indigenous peoples have to contend with while others, like Witi Ihimaera's "Life As It Really Is", undermine stereotypes and critique the ways in which Indigenous peoples and our cultures have been portrayed in mainstream media.

Alootook Ipellie's "Love Triangle", Maria Campbell's "Dah Teef" and Joseph Bruchac's "The Hungry One" honour and affirm traditional forms, styles, and characters, while Louise Erdrich, Kenny Laughton, Linda Hogan, and Richard Van Camp's stories bring old time knowledge into contemporary situations. In its sensitive and unflinching portrayal of the impact of AIDS, Richard Van Camp's story is among the most provocative, moving, and contemporary in the collection. Melissa Lucashenko's story "let me tell you what I want" is also provocative and contemporary and, in its exploration and portrayal of Aboriginal love and sexuality, perhaps more than any other will forever destroy any limitations, stereotypes or preconceived ideas others might place on what Indigenous writing ought to be.

What may be most surprising, however, is that although many of the stories are about great tragedies, injustices, and losses, the majority of them are also quite funny. The role of humour in the work of Indigenous writers is complex and reflects a significant aspect of our cultures. The stories in *skins*, like the greatest storytellers in our traditions and like the greatest of any literary tradition, can transport you in such a way that you will experience the full range of human emotion before you finish. By turns sad, enraging, angry, joyful, tragic, and humorous, these stories will leave you richer, more inspired, and far more knowledgeable about Indigenous literature and culture than you were before.

Although full and satisfying, this collection is a small taste of the bounty of Indigenous contemporary writing. In presenting you with this collection we hope you will enjoy it and that you will hunger for more.

N'd'nawaendaugunuk,

Kateri Akiwenzie-Damm

Mirrored Images

Aboriginal writing has gone beyond the need for definition, and it has always been defined for us anyway, perhaps as a way of making our writing fit the mainstream perception of Aboriginal literature, of why Aboriginal people write. The short stories in *skins, contemporary Indigenous writing* speak for themselves, they take on a life of their own, and they defy imposed literary constructs. In *skins* the writers cross the international borders of Australia, Aotearoa, Canada and the United States, at the same time bringing together shared histories and experiences.

The writing in *skins* represents a freedom and diversity of voice, storyline, style and character — a freedom that is not often reflected in the social, economic or political realities of our urban and remote communities. Aboriginal writing has a history built on censure — censure of our culture, language and artistic practices. Early Aboriginal writing came from the necessity of political activism and while there is no denying that Aboriginal writing today has evolved from this, the stories in *skins* don't all necessarily have a blatant message. What they do is open the reader up to an emotion, a feeling, an insight into Aboriginal culture, the subtleties of Aboriginal humour, irony and expression and our adaptation and usage of English alongside our own languages.

In compiling and editing *skins*, Kateri and I hope to introduce Aboriginal writers to the writing of others outside their own nations as well as bringing them to the attention of a more general readership. The anthology is a compilation of successful and acclaimed writers who have made a difference and who continue to make a difference. They challenge mainstream perceptions of Aboriginal literature, but also challenge our own communities and cultures by holding up a mirror to the spoken and unspoken realities of our own lives.

Josie Douglas

First Nations and Inuit

Canada

Dah Teef

Maria Campbell

You know
me I talk about dah whitemans like dere dah only
ones dat steal.
But dats not true you know
cause some of our own peoples dey steal too.

Oh yeah dats true
We gots some damn good teefs among us
an dah worse ting about dem
is dey steal from us dere very own peoples.

I member a man one time
dat was a teef.
Boy he was a bad one too.
At firs
he wasen very good at it
an he gets caught all dah time.

Later
when he goes away from our village
he becomes perfessional
an he gets real good.
But dah peoples dey knowed it was him
cause he already build a repetation as one.

He use to steal every damn ting dat man.
He jus can be choosey.

He never gets good enough to steal land dough.
Maybe it cause we don gots any to steal by den
and he gots no practice.
But boy
he shore got good at stealing everyting else.

One time you know dis ole man
we call him Geebow.
He have a nice hat.
Hoo, he was real fancy.
A black one
dah kine da old Breeds dey really like.
Hees got a silk embroder hatban wit a falcon fedder
stuck on it.
Dat falcon fedder you know
he was old Geebow hees spirit
an he help him all hees life.

Well one day
dis ole Geebow he go visit Margareet.
Margareet him
he was an ole widow woman dat Geebow he like.

When he gets to hees house
dat ole lady he have a nice meal all cook
an he ask him to stay.
You know
dat ole man he never take hees hat off nearly all hees life
but when Margareet he ask him to eat
he take it off.
Dat ole Geebow
he gots good manners
like all dah ole peoples dey use to have.

Well on dis day
dis man dat was dah teef
he come visiting too.
Dat man he always knowed where dah good meals dey was.
Boy
I like to use hees name
but I can do dat cause he wouldn be right
An me
I don want to make hees granchildren suffer
cause dere all good peoples.
Hees not dere fault dat dere granfawder he pick dat
way to make a name for hisself.

Anyways
dah teef he come visiting
and Margareet him
he wasen very happy bout dat cause dat mean him and
Geebow
dey can be alone.
But Margareet him
he was a good woman
So he ask him to eat wit dem
an he watch him real clos so he don steal nutting.

Dere wasen very much he can steal from dah table
anyways
'cept dah knifes and forks.
An Margareet he knowed he wouldn dare take dem
cause dat woman you know
hees got a hell of a repetation for being a hardheaded woman
when he gets mad.
Dat man he have to be a damn fool to steal from
hees table.

So dey sit down to eat
Margareet ole Geebow an dah teef.
An dey make good talk at dah table like civilize
peoples.
Hoo, he was a hell of a meal to.

Dat woman he was a good cook
an he really done hees bes for ole Geebow.
When dey finish eating
dah teef he jump up an he say he gots to go.
"I got to talk business wit a Frenchman called
Bilado"
He say.
Den he tank Margareet and he go.

When he leave
Margareet he check all hees knifes and forks.
Dey was all dere
but Margareet he still don trust him.
"Someting hees not right"
Margareet he say to Geebow.
"Hees not like dat man to leave when he knowed I got raisen pie."

"By golly"
Ole Geebow he say
"Maybe dah Prees he finely talk some sense into him."

Dem ole peoples
dey feel real good dat nutting he was missing
an maybe
dat man he change hees ways.

Dey visit till late at night
an ole Geebow him

he finely get dah courage to ask Margareet to marry him.
Margareet he say yes
cause hees been waiting damn near twenty years for
dat ole man to ask him.

Ooh dey have a good visit after dat.
Dey kiss
an dey talk about dah wedding dere gonna have.
Ole Geebow him
hees never been married before an he wan to have a
big wedding.
He wants dah high mass
and everyting dat go wit it.
Margareet he like dat
cause now he can wear a long dress. He can do dat
dah firs time cause he was too poor.
Dat Margareet
he was a rich woman now cause hees husban
he use to be a big farmer
an he leave him all hees money.
Course him
he deserve dat money cause he done damn near all dah work.

But anyways dat ole Geebow
he was damn lucky dat woman he love him
an he wan to marry him.

Well finely he was eleven o'clock
time for ole Geebow to go home.
In dem days you know
nobody wit any sense he walk home at midnight or after
cause dere liable to run into a Rou Garou on dah road.
Oh yeah!
Dat road he was famous for Rou Garous.

An ole Geebow him
he might be pour an all dat
but he gots lots of good sense.

But den
he can stay wit Margareet eeder
cause in dem days
peoples dey don sleep wit each udder until dere married.

Margareet and Geebow dey was real ole time peoples dat
believe on dah right way
So Geebow him
he get up to leave.
He give Margareet a kiss
den he go for hees hat an he can fine it.
Dey look all over but he was gone.
Dat damn teef you know
he steal dat hat.
Ole Geebow him
he nearly have a broken heart
Dat hat he means a lot to him.
An besides
he tinks dats why Margareet he look at him dah first time.
Cause hee gots a smart hat.

An hees falcon fedder
hees granmudder he gave it to him when he was a young man
an he only wear it for very special.
Like dis night
he was very special.

Well by dah time him an dah ole lady
dey finish looking for it
he was after midnight an Geebow

he can go home cause of dah Rou Garous.
An deres no damn way Margareet hees gonna let him go eeder.
He don want no Rou Garou to take hees man.
So
he tell him to stay
an he make him a bed on dah floor.

Boy dat teef!
He jus make it hard on dem ole peoples.

Dere was only one big room in Margareet hees house an when dey go to bed
Margareet
he can take hees close off cause Geebow him hees
on dah floor.

An Margareet him
he don know what dat ole man he'll do if he sees
hees pettycoats.
Dat teef
he jus cause a bunch of trouble.

Well you know
when dah morning he comes
Geebow he wake up cause he hear somebody knocking on
dah door.
He never even tink
he jus jump up an he open dah door
an dere was Margareet hees granson Guspar wit dah
neighbour dere boy.
Guspar he was surprise
an kine of shame to
cause hees granmudder he have a man in hees house.
Dats not dah kine of ting
a boy he like to tink hees granmudder he do.

Well ole Geebow an Margareet
dey done dah bes dey could to tell dem boys what he happen
but dat neighbour boy
he go home an he tell hees mudder what he see
an dat woman
hees got a big mout an he tell everybody
An pretty soon
dah story of Geebow an Margareet sleeping togedder he
gets all over.
So dem ole peoples
dey gots to get married as fas as the Prees he allow dem.
An everybody
he say Margareet an Geebow dey have a shotgun wedding.

Well he wasen true.
How you can have a shotgun wedding when your over
seventy years ole?
Dats how ole dey was.

But you know what our peoples dere like.
Talking an teasing all dah time.
Ole Geebow him
he kine of like dat
cause dat kine of talk make him feel young.

But he worry about Margareet hees repetation
cause you know
dat Margareet
he was a good Catlic woman
an he would of never have a shotgun wedding
Even if he was young.

Boy dat teef
he shore cause a hell of a ruckus in dah village.

An you know
ole Geebow he never get hees hat back
But he fine hees fedder.
He was stuck on hees door frame one day when he come home.

Some people dey say
dat dah teef
he at lees have a little respec cause he don keep
dat fedder.
But me
I know damn well why he bring it back.

Everybody in our part of dah country
knows dat Geebow him
he know Indian medicine.

Dey know to
dat fedder he was Geebows spirit.

Dat teef
he was jus damn scare when he saw what he took
dats why he bring it back.
Not because he have respec
cause dat man he never have any.

Well you know
dat teef he never change hees ways.
All hees life he steal.
He never work for a living like everybody else he do.
He have a good woman too
an a hell of a pile of kids.
Dey all turn out good dough
but dats cause hees wife he teach dem dah good way.

Hees not just dah stealing dats bad you know.
All dough dats bad enough.
Dah real bad ting is your kids and all your granchildren.
Dey don got no good stories about you if your a teef.

An dah stories you know
dats dah bes treasure of all to leave your family.
Everyting else on dis eart
he gets los or wore out.
But dah stories dey las forever.
Too bad about dat man hees kids.
Jus too bad.

Love Triangle

Alootook Ipellie

In small, isolated camps, relationships between my fellow Inuit were sometimes precarious. For the most part, all of us tolerated our life-long relationships because it was the only way we could survive. And only out of necessity, did we go to extremes to solve disagreements and rifts between certain members of our camp.

For me as a shaman, one of my functions was to help sworn enemies reach reconciliation. Some of these conflicts sometimes reached crisis proportions which, unfortunately, I could not do anything about before fatalities occurred. But most times, I was successful in healing bruised egos and initiating the rebirth of cordiality between hearts and minds.

One summer, the weather was unusually hot, made hotter by an on-going feud between two men from our camp. One, named Ossuk, was a handsome young man who had recently moved in from another camp with his family. The other, Nalikkaaq, was an older man married to a beautiful woman, Aqaqa. Unbeknownst to Nalikkaaq, Ossuk had been having an affair with Aqaqa. It was by pure coincidence that Nalikkaaq found out about their amorous relationship.

One day, when Nalikkaaq was out on the sea on his qayaq hunting for seal, a snow bunting landed on the bow of his qayaq and started bantering on about Ossuk and Aqaqa. Nalikkaaq couldn't believe what he was hearing from the snow bunting.

Although the weather was perfect for seal hunting that day, Nalikkaaq could no more concentrate on the task at hand and kept missing seal after seal even at close range. Ossuk's face kept getting in the way of his number one priority and that was to bring back the much-needed seal to his family. He eventually lost all patience and headed back to camp determined to get at the throat of Ossuk.

When he arrived at the camp, he went straight to his tent to confront his wife. Madness had taken hold of him and in his rage, he only grunted and mumbled unrecognizable words. Aqaqa could only shrug and continue her sewing.

"What is it you want to say?" Aqaqa asked Nalikkaaq. "Did you bring me seal?"

Nalikkaaq opened his mouth and tried once again but failed. He had to sit on the platform bed beside Aqaqa to calm down.

After a time, Nalikkaaq was calm enough to say the first words of inquiry into the alleged affair.

"Ossuk..." Nalikkaaq hesitated. "Ossuk...I hear, has been visiting your private parts. Is this true? Aqaqa, enlighten me, please!"

"Ossuk? Who is Ossuk? I have never heard of Ossuk. Who do you mean to speak of? Who is Ossuk?"

"I was out in the middle of the sea and this little snow bunting landed on my qayaq and told me the whole story about you and Ossuk. Don't try to deny anything with me, Aqaqa. I have heard it all...that you two have been entertaining each other for many days while I was out doing my husbandly chores to bring food to your side. Come on, Aqaqa, admit that you have betrayed me. Admit!"

"Nalikkaaq, Nalikkaaq...please give me the privilege of denying anything to do with Ossuk. Ossuk is a stranger in my life. I have never heard of Ossuk. I have never seen anyone by the name of Ossuk. Nalikkaaq, I plead with you to believe me when I say I have never had the privilege of being entertained by or to entertain a fictional man named Ossuk."

"But the snow bunting...is a messenger I have trusted for a lifetime. It knows what it speaks of. It spoke of amorous liaisons between the two of you. Don't deny this now, Aqaqa. Don't deny. Don't deny!"

"Nalikkaaq, I deny, I deny. And that is it."

Nalikkaaq decided to drop the inquiry for the moment. He had better things to do than to be stonewalled by his own wife about the rumour of her amorous interludes with Ossuk. He got up and went out of the tent. He looked down to the water's edge and spotted Ossuk preparing his qayaq to paddle out on a hunt. Nalikkaaq ran down to meet Ossuk. His curiosity was getting the better of him. He just had to get to the bottom of the wild rumour brought about by the snow bunting.

"Ossuk, are you about to go seal hunting?"

"Yes, Nalikkaaq. That is the purpose of my preparation."

"You mind if I join you? You see, I was out hunting earlier and did not bring back any seal for my wife and children. Maybe I will have better luck hunting with you."

"Fine. Suits me. One never knows when we might run into beluga whales. We must always be prepared for that."

In due time, Nalikkaaq and Ossuk paddled out together into the open sea. The wind was so calm, the sun bright with energy. A perfect day for hunting wild game.

They paddled for a long time until their camp was out of sight. Nalikkaaq raged secretly in his mind and heart. Somehow he kept everything to himself. But he knew he could explode any moment. The thought of Ossuk entering the private parts of his wife Aqaqa drove him on the brink of striking Ossuk in the back with the beluga whale harpoon. He was in a perfect position to do so, paddling slightly behind. He could do it at any moment, if he wanted to. However, he hesitated several times, knowing full well that one strike in the back would not guarantee a fatal blow. He was afraid that Ossuk would end up retaliating, and then he, Nalikkaaq, would be the one killed instead of Ossuk. The safer plan would be to wait until they went ashore somewhere. He would then be more certain of killing Ossuk.

Nalikkaaq decided to concentrate on finding and hunting seals that were so urgently needed in camp. Killing a human could wait. It wasn't long before a seal popped up from under the surface of the water to breathe. Nalikkaaq and Ossuk paddled towards it, harpoons ready. In time, the seal popped up once again very close to their qayaqs. Nalikkaaq and Ossuk hurled their harpoons, both stabbing the seal at the same time. There was a minor dispute as to which of them had hit it first. In a situation like this, it was custom to give the older man credit for the kill. Nalikkaaq smiled ear to ear. The seal was on its way to his wife and family. He was a happy man.

It wasn't long before another seal popped up and Nalikkaaq had thoughts of picking up the beluga whale harpoon instead of the seal harpoon. He was again imagining Ossuk embracing his beautiful wife Aqaqa, and, God forbid, in his own tent! The two of them paddled in the direction of the seal. Nalikkaaq had decided this was the moment he would make Ossuk pay for his dire deeds. He readied the beluga whale harpoon to be fatally plunged into the flesh of Ossuk. However, Ossuk was a very perceptive young man. He noticed Nalikkaaq holding the beluga whale harpoon.

"Nalikkaaq, why are you using the beluga whale harpoon when there aren't any belugas around?"

"Ossuk, I just wanted to make sure the little seal died instantly with this larger harpoon. I have had experiences with seals escaping my seal harpoon because it wasn't powerful enough. This is the reason why."

"You know, as well as I, Nalikkaaq, that it is a bad omen to use a beluga whale harpoon on a seal. It will only bring you bad luck. You must respect the seal, and using the beluga whale harpoon means you do not respect it."

"You are so bloody right, Ossuk. I forgot. I wasn't thinking."

Nalikkaaq had no choice but to put away the beluga whale harpoon. He felt a little embarrassed by the young man since he was considered the elder and should, in the eyes of Ossuk, have known better. Nalikkaaq quickly reverted back to his seal harpoon and paddled on. He felt incensed by Ossuk's very presence. He was boiling inside.

The seal popped up again to the right of Ossuk. Nalikkaaq could hardly see it. He went for it anyway as Ossuk easily plunged his harpoon into the hapless seal. Nalikkaaq's harpoon had misfired and strayed into Ossuk's qayaq, puncturing it. The hole was far enough from the water surface that it didn't spring a leak. Nalikkaaq's embarrassment turned into a feeling of humiliation. As he paddled close to Ossuk's qayaq to retrieve his harpoon, Nalikkaaq came up with an idea. The plan was to hit Ossuk's qayaq again, this time under the water surface so it would leak and drown this despicable adulterer.

"Please, Ossuk, forgive me for hitting your qayaq. The rope got tangled in my fingers as I released it. It was entirely accidental. I apologize."

"Accidents do happen, Nalikkaaq. Accidents do happen."

Ossuk pulled the seal onto his qayaq and prepared to paddle to the shore to butcher the seal. He was so hungry for it.

"Nalikkaaq, will you join me for a little feast on the shore?"

"I cannot refuse such an offer. I am famished for seal meat and blubber. And especially for warm blood."

Nalikkaaq was salivating as he paddled toward the land. The sinking and drowning of Ossuk would have to wait. Warm blood was all that was on his mind. Warm blood, not just of the seal, but also the warm blood flowing out of Ossuk's body.

It wasn't long before they landed on shore. Ossuk hauled his seal on top of a smooth rock. He began cutting the seal from just under its chin and down to its flippers as if he was unzipping it. The carcass steamed. Its blood was indeed still quite warm. Nalikkaaq crouched over the seal, cupped his palms and sunk them into the warm blood and sucked the blood with fervour.

"Such a heavenly drink!" Nalikkaaq celebrated, his lips coloured in crimson. "Nothing quite like it compares! Let me at its liver!"

Nalikkaaq retrieved his knife and cut out the liver. Then he cut off some blubber and ate it with the liver, mouthfuls at a time.

Nalikkaaq looked up toward the sky and put his arms up to acknowledge the Creator and said, "This is food for the gods. Thank you. Thank you. Thank you."

Ossuk wasn't saying much. He went about the business of filling himself. His appetite was fierce.

"What a blessed land we live in!" Nalikkaaq bellowed out. His voice echoed against the side of a mountain across the fiord. "It is at these moments we rejoice the bounty of this great land!"

"Indeed Nalikkaaq, indeed," smiled Ossuk, gobbling seal flesh down his throat.

Nalikkaaq had forgotten about the rumour of Ossuk and Aqaqa's sexual trysts until the knife in his hand began reminding him of its uses other than cutting up seal meat. His vengeful self re-emerged from the depth of his mind. "I can end it all now," he thought as he looked at Ossuk's busy throat.

Soon the little feast was over. Ossuk put holes alongside where he had slit the seal and closed the carcass by looping the holes with rope and put the seal back on his qayaq. Nalikkaaq cleaned his knife in the salt water and imagined it slicing up Ossuk. "An adulterer deserves no dignity while alive," he thought.

"Ossuk, did I tell you about the story of a bloody feud between two powerful shamans over the wife of one of the shamans?"

"No," Ossuk nodded.

"As the story was related to me some time ago, one of the shamans had committed adultery with the other shaman's wife and a bloody feud ensued for many hours in a camp. The camp members were given the most frightening show of their lives. It turned out that the two of them bared their chests and fought the wrestling match of their lives. The bloody feud ended when one of the shamans took hold of the adulterer's penis and swung him around in mid-air four or five times and, the poor man, his penis and testicles were ripped right off his crotch! The penisless shaman managed to survive the ordeal but he was never to penetrate the private parts of a woman again, least of all, the winning shaman's wife. It was a horrendous spectacle, made more so when the shaman looked at the severed penis and testicles in his hand and then flung them violently out to sea. They floated off to kingdom come."

"Ouch," Ossuk cringed his face. "That's one of the most disgusting stories I've ever heard. Are you making it up?"

"Of course not. I think the adulterer got exactly what he deserved. Don't you think so?"

"According to the winning shaman, I suppose. What a way to be castrated. It hurts in the crotch just thinking about it. Would you have done that yourself if you found out that another man had been having an affair with your wife?"

"To give you an honest opinion, under the circumstances, I would probably do it."

"Gruesome..."

"Ossuk, can I ask you a personal question?"

"Yes, as long as it's within the bounds of decency, I will try to answer it."

"Have you ever committed adultery?"

"Never."

"Ossuk, that's a lie. Earlier today, I was visited by a little snow bunting who spilled out you and Aqaqa's best-kept secret. The snow bunting revealed to me that you two had been having secret liaisons. Isn't that right?"

"A little snow bunting?" Ossuk gave out a nervous laugh. "What a likely story. A pack of lies. Are you out of your mind, Nalikkaaq? It's a pack of incredible lies!"

"Don't deny, Ossuk. Don't you deny!"

"Pack of lies! Pack of lies! Pack of lies!" Ossuk yelled at Nalikkaaq and started to push his qayaq into the water. He jumped into it and was soon racing toward the camp. He was determined to get away from his accuser as quickly as possible.

Nalikkaaq jumped into his qayaq and paddled after Ossuk. "So, Ossuk is paddling away from the truth!" He soon caught up to Ossuk. There they were, paddling side by side, one mouthing off vindictives, the other vehemently denying his accuser's words. The two men seemed like they were in an Olympic qayaq race as they skimmed at great speed through the calm sea.

"You'll pay for this!" Nalikkaaq yelled at Ossuk. They were nearing their camp. The people in camp heard and saw what was happening and watched the two qayaqers coming to land on the shore. They went down to find out what the commotion was all about.

Ossuk and Nalikkaaq simultaneously jumped out of their qayaqs. Nalikkaaq immediately went over to confront Ossuk. "You are a dirty little adulterer!" Nalikkaaq yelled pointing an index finger at Ossuk. "Let everyone know this dirty little truth! Ossuk, you cannot deny it any more!"

The people were a little shocked that something like this was taking place right in front of their faces. They looked at each other in utter amazement. Nalikkaaq was pushing Ossuk's chest and shoulders. "Dirt!" he yelled. "Dirt!"

I walked over to the two feuding men and told them to calm down. "You are men who are capable of reasoning with each other and a fight like this will not solve any of your troubles. So, I suggest a wrestling match between the two of you. Right here and now."

"Fair enough," Nalikkaaq immediately agreed.

However, Ossuk was hesitant. "I am an innocent man facing a false accusation of committing adultery with Aqaqa! I will not submit to such false pressure! Nalikkaaq, take your unfounded accusations and anger elsewhere!"

"Wait! Wait! Wait!" Aqaqa came running down to the shore from her tent. Everyone looked around to see a frantic Aqaqa with her sewing still in hand. "I have a confession to make!" Aqaqa stopped and caught up with her breath. "Nalikkaaq, the amorous rendezvous between me and Ossuk did happen. I have fallen in love with the man of my dreams." Aqaqa turned to her lover. "Ossuk, do not deny it any more. Let the truth be known. Confess! Confess! Confess!"

Ossuk was in a state of shock, mouth agape. "What are you saying, Aqaqa? What are you saying?"

"Let the truth be known, and I have said it."

Ossuk wasn't going to admit to anything, but everyone now knew the truth. Nalikkaaq could hardly contain his anger. "Enough!" he yelled and lunged at Ossuk.

"Nooo!" I yelled at Nalikkaaq and went between the two men. "Reason shall prevail. A wrestling match is in order. It is our ancient method of solving disputes and depressurizing a raging mind. Nalikkaaq and Ossuk, bare your chests."

"So be it," Ossuk succumbed to the pressure. At any rate, he would not back down from a challenge. He had the advantage of being younger and stronger than Nalikkaaq. He would rely on those qualities, if he could, to defeat Nalikkaaq.

The Arctic Wrestling Federation Championship Match was on. The women cried out of fear. The children held onto their mothers and shuffled their feet on the ground. The men yelled in excitement.

Nalikkaaq and Ossuk were almost a perfect match at the beginning. They would take turns lifting and slamming each other on the ground, to thunderous applause mostly from the men, cries of fear from the women, to wondrous curiosity from the children.

At one point, Nalikkaaq went after Ossuk's throat and almost choked him to death until Ossuk was able to knee Nalikkaaq in the crotch and release his hands just in time. There was a short pause in the struggle as Nalikkaaq clutched his crotch with both hands and Ossuk coughed out the effects of his near-choking.

"Come on, you wretched men!" A man yelled out from the crowd. "We're not here to watch a bore-off! Get on with it!"

Aqaqa was unusually calm about what was happening in front of her. Perhaps it had something to do with her confidence in Ossuk, her lover, that his youth and strength would eventually prevail over the aging body of her husband, Nalikkaaq.

Aqaqa underestimated one thing, her husband's experience and maturity. Nalikkaaq was deft at checks and balances, leverages and angles that one acquired only with experience. He had practised wrestling holds for years and was exceptionally good at deception. He had plenty of moves that mesmerized the lesser-experienced Ossuk.

"No! No! No!" Aqaqa yelled as Nalikkaaq suddenly got hold of Ossuk's penis and began swinging him around in mid-air. "No! No! No!" she yelled again.

"Aaaahhhh!" cried Ossuk as Nalikkaaq threw him to the ground, minus his penis and testicles! Then Nalikkaaq looked at the severed parts and threw them out to sea, bellowing out obscenities.

Aqaqa became hysterical, crying on her knees looking over Ossuk.

What Nalikkaaq hadn't told Ossuk earlier was that he was the shaman who had ripped off the penis of the other shaman! Now he had done it again, this time to the hapless Ossuk.

In Nalikkaaq's world, three's a crowd.

Borders

Thomas King

When I was twelve, maybe thirteen, my mother announced that we were going to go to Salt Lake City to visit my sister who had left the reserve, moved across the line, and found a job. Laetitia had not left home with my mother's blessing, but over time my mother had come to be proud of the fact that Laetitia had done all of this on her own.

"She did real good," my mother would say.

Then there were the fine points to Laetitia's going. She had not, as my mother liked to tell Mrs. Manyfingers, gone floating after some man like a balloon on a string. She hadn't snuck out of the house, either, and gone to Vancouver or Edmonton or Toronto to chase rainbows down alleys. And she hadn't been pregnant.

"She did real good."

I was seven or eight when Laetitia left home. She was seventeen. Our father was from Rocky Boy on the American side.

"Dad's American," Laetitia told my mother, "so I can go and come as I please."

"Send us a postcard."

Laetitia packed her things, and we headed for the border. Just outside of Milk River, Laetitia told us to watch for the water tower.

"Over the next rise. It's the first thing you see."

"We got a water tower on the reserve," my mother said. "There's a big one in Lethbridge, too."

"You'll be able to see the tops of the flagpoles, too. That's where the border is."

When we got to Coutts, my mother stopped at the convenience store and bought her and Laetitia a cup of coffee. I got an Orange Crush.

"This is real lousy coffee."

"You're just angry because I want to see the world."

"It's the water. From here on down, they got lousy water."

"I can catch the bus from Sweetgrass. You don't have to lift a finger."

"You're going to have to buy your water in bottles if you want good coffee."

There was an old wooden building about a block away, with a tall sign in the yard that said "Museum." Most of the roof had been blown away. Mom told me to go and see when the place was open. There were boards over the windows and doors. You could tell that the place was closed, and I told Mom so, but she said to go and check anyway. Mom and Laetitia stayed by the car. Neither one of them moved. I sat down on the steps of the museum and watched them, and I don't know that they ever said anything to each other. Finally, Laetitia got her bag out of the trunk and gave Mom a hug.

I wandered back to the car. The wind had come up, and it blew Laetitia's hair across her face. Mom reached out and pulled the strands out of Laetitia's eyes, and Laetitia let her.

"You can still see the mountain from here," my mother told Laetitia in Blackfoot.

"Lots of mountains in Salt Lake," Laetitia told her in English.

"The place is closed," I said. "Just like I told you."

Laetitia tucked her hair into her jacket and dragged her bag down the road to the brick building with the American flag flapping on a pole. When she got to where the guards were waiting, she turned, put the bag down, and waved to us. We waved back. Then my mother turned the car around, and we came home.

We got postcards from Laetitia regular, and, if she wasn't spreading jelly on the truth, she was happy. She found a good job and rented an apartment with a pool.

"And she can't even swim," my mother told Mrs. Manyfingers.

Most of the postcards said we should come down and see the city, but whenever I mentioned this, my mother would stiffen up.

So I was surprised when she bought two new tires for the car and put on her blue dress with the green and yellow flowers. I had to dress up, too, for my mother did not want us crossing the border looking like Americans. We made sandwiches and put them in a big box with pop and potato chips and some apples and bananas and a big jar of water.

"But we can stop at one of those restaurants, too, right?"

"We maybe should take some blankets in case you get sleepy."

"But we can stop at one of those restaurants, too, right?"

The border was actually two towns, though neither one was big enough to amount to anything. Coutts was on the Canadian side and consisted of the convenience store and gas station, the museum that was closed and boarded up, and a motel. Sweetgrass was on the American side, but all you could see was an overpass that arched across the highway and disappeared into the prairies. Just hearing the names of these towns, you would expect that Sweetgrass, which is a nice name and sounds like it is related to other places such as Medicine Hat and Moose Jaw and Kicking Horse Pass, would be on the Canadian side, and that Coutts, which sounds abrupt and rude, would be on the American side. But this was not the case.

Between the two borders was a duty-free shop where you could buy cigarettes and liquor and flags. Stuff like that.

We left the reserve in the morning and drove until we got to Coutts.

"Last time we stopped here," my mother said, "you had an Orange Crush. You remember that?"

"Sure," I said. "That was when Laetitia took off."

"You want another Orange Crush?"

"That means we're not going to stop at a restaurant, right?"

My mother got a coffee at the convenience store, and we stood around and watched the prairies move in the sunlight. Then we climbed back in the car. My mother straightened the dress across her thighs, leaned against the wheel, and drove all the way to the border in first gear, slowly, as if she were trying to see through a bad storm or riding high on black ice.

The border guard was an old guy. As he walked to the car, he swayed from side to side, his feet set wide apart, the holster on his hip pitching up and down. He leaned into the window, looked into the back seat, and looked at my mother and me.

"Morning, ma'am."

"Good morning."

"Where you heading?"

"Salt Lake City."

"Purpose of your visit?"

"Visit my daughter."

"Citizenship?"

"Blackfoot," my mother told him.

"Ma'am?"

"Blackfoot," my mother repeated.

"Canadian?"

"Blackfoot."

It would have been easier if my mother had just said "Canadian" and been done with it, but I could see she wasn't going to do that. The guard wasn't angry or anything. He smiled and looked towards the building. Then he turned back and nodded.

"Morning ma'am."

"Good morning."

"Any firearms or tobacco?"

"No."

"Citizenship?"

"Blackfoot."

He told us to sit in the car and wait, and we did. In about five minutes, another guard came out with the first man. They were talking as they came, both men swaying back and forth like two cowboys headed for a bar or a gunfight.

"Morning ma'am."

"Good morning."

"Cecil tells me you and the boys are Blackfoot."

"That's right."

"Now, I know that we got Blackfeet on the American side and the Canadians got Blackfeet on their side. Just so we can keep our records straight, what side do you come from?"

I knew exactly what my mother was going to say, and I could have told them if they had asked me.

"Canadian side or American side?" asked the guard.

"Blackfoot side," she said.

It didn't take them long to lose their sense of humor, I can tell you that. The one guard stopped smiling altogether and told us to park our car at the side of the building and come in.

We sat on a wood bench for about an hour before anyone came over to talk to us. This time it was a woman. She had a gun, too.

"Hi," she said. "I'm Inspector Pratt. I understand there is a little misunderstanding."

"I'm going to visit my daughter in Salt Lake City," my mother told her. "We don't have any guns or beer."

"It's a legal technicality, that's all."

"My daughter's Blackfoot, too."

The woman opened a briefcase and took out a couple of forms and began to write on one of them. "Everyone who crosses our border has to declare their citizenship. Even Americans. It helps us keep track of the visitors we get from the various countries."

She went on like that for maybe fifteen minutes, and a lot of the stuff she told us was interesting.

"I can understand how you feel about having to tell us your citizenship, and here's what I'll do. You tell me, and I won't put it down on the form. No-one will know but you and me."

Her gun was silver. There were several chips in the wood handle and the name "Stella" was scratched into the metal butt.

We were in the border office for about four hours, and we talked to almost everyone there. One of the men bought me a Coke. My mother brought a couple of sandwiches in from the car. I offered part of mine to Stella, but she said she wasn't hungry.

I told Stella that we were Blackfoot and Canadian, but she said that that didn't count because I was a minor. In the end, she told us that if my mother didn't declare her citizenship, we would have to go back to where we came from. My mother stood up and thanked Stella for her time. Then we got back in the car and drove to the Canadian border, which was only about a hundred yards away.

I was disappointed. I hadn't seen Laetitia for a long time, and I had never been to Salt Lake City. When she was still at home, Laetitia would go on and on about Salt Lake City. She had never been there, but her boyfriend Lester Tallbull had spent a year in Salt Lake City at a technical school.

"It's a great place," Lester would say. "Nothing but blondes in the whole state."

Whenever he said that, Laetitia would slug him on his shoulder hard enough to make him flinch. He had some brochures on Salt Lake and some maps, and every so often the two of them would spread them out on the table.

"That's the temple. It's right downtown. You got to have a pass to get in."

"Charlotte says anyone can go in and look around."

"When was Charlotte in Salt Lake? Just when the hell was Charlotte in Salt Lake?"

"Last year."

"This is Liberty Park. It's got a zoo. There's good skiing in the mountains."

"Got all the skiing we can use," my mother would say. "People come from all over the world to ski at Banff. Cardston's got a temple, if you like those things."

"Oh, this one is real big," Lester would say. "They got armed guards and everything."

"Not what Charlotte says."

"What does she know?"

Lester and Laetitia broke up, but I guess the idea of Salt Lake stuck in her mind.

The Canadian border guard was a young woman, and she seemed happy to see us. "Hi," she said. "You folks sure have a great day for a trip. Where are you coming from?"

"Standoff."

"Is that in Montana?"

"No."

"Where are you going?"

"Standoff."

The woman's name was Carol and I don't guess she was any older than Laetitia. "Wow, you both Canadians?"

"Blackfoot."

"Really? I have a friend I went to school with who is Blackfoot. Do you know Mike Harley?"

"No."

"He went to school in Lethbridge, but he's really from Browning."

It was a nice conversation and there were no cars behind us, so there was no rush.

"You're not bringing any liquor back, are you?"

"No."

"Any cigarettes or plants or stuff like that?"

"No."

"Citizenship?"

"Blackfoot."

"I know," said the woman, "and I'd be proud of being Blackfoot if I were Blackfoot. But you have to be American or Canadian."

When Laetitia and Lester broke up, Lester took his brochures and maps with him, so Laetitia wrote to someone in Salt Lake City, and, about a month later, she got a big envelope of stuff. We sat at the table and opened up all the brochures, and Laetitia read each one out loud.

"Salt Lake City is a gateway to some of the world's most magnificent skiing.

"Salt Lake City is the home of one of the natural wonders of the world."

It was kind of exciting seeing all those colour brochures on the table and listening to Laetitia read all about how Salt Lake City was one of the best places in the entire world.

"That Salt Lake city place sounds too good to be true," my mother told her.

"It has everything."

"We got everything right here."

"It's boring here."

"People in Salt Lake City are probably sending away for brochures of Calgary and Lethbridge and Pincher Creek right now."

In the end, my mother would say that maybe Laetitia should go to Salt Lake City, and Laetitia would say that maybe she would.

We parked the car to the side of the building and Carol led us into a small room on the second floor. I found a comfortable spot on the couch and flipped through some back issues of *Saturday Night* and *Alberta Report*.

When I woke up, my mother was just coming out of another office. She didn't say a word to me. I followed her down the stairs and out to the car. I thought we were going home, but she turned the car around and drove back towards the American border, which made me think we were going to visit Laetitia in Salt Lake City after all. Instead she pulled into the parking lot of the duty-free store and stopped.

"We going to see Laetitia?"

"No."

"We going home?"

Pride is a good thing to have, you know. Laetitia had a lot of pride, and so did my mother. I figured that someday, I'd have it too.

"So where are we going?"

Most of that day, we wandered around the duty-free store, which wasn't very large. The manager had a name tag with a tiny American flag on one side and a tiny Canadian flag on the other. His name was Mel. Towards evening he started suggesting we should be on our way. I told him we had nowhere to go, that neither the Americans nor the Canadians would let us in. He laughed at that and told us that we should buy something or leave.

The car was not very comfortable, but we did have all that food and it was April, so even if it did snow as it sometimes does on the prairies, we wouldn't freeze. The next morning my mother drove to the American border.

It was a different guard this time, but the questions were the same. We didn't spend as much time in the office as we did the day before. By noon, we were back at the Canadian border. By two we were back in the duty-free shop parking lot.

The second night in the car was not as much fun as the first, but my mother seemed in good spirits, and, all in all, it was as much an adventure as an inconvenience. There wasn't much food left and that was a problem, but we had lots of water as there was a faucet at the side of the duty-free shop.

One Sunday, Laetitia and I were watching television. Mom was over at Mrs. Manyfingers'. Right in the middle of the program, Laetitia turned off the set and said she was going to Salt Lake City, that life around here was too boring. I had wanted to see the rest of the program and really didn't care if Laetitia went to Salt Lake City or not. When Mom got home, I told her what Laetitia had said.

What surprised me was how angry Laetitia got when she found out that I had told Mom.

"You got a big mouth."

"That's what you said."

"What I said is none of your business."

"I didn't say anything."

"Well, I'm going for sure, now."

That weekend, Laetitia packed her bags, and we drove her to the border.

Mel turned out to be friendly. When he closed up for the night and found us still parked in the lot, he came over and asked us if our car was broken down or something. My mother thanked him for his concern and told him we were fine, that things would get straightened out in the morning.

"You're kidding," said Mel. "You'd think they could handle the simple things."

"We got some apples and a banana," I said, "but we're all out of ham sandwiches."

"You know, you read about these things, but you just don't believe it. You just don't believe it."

"Hamburgers would be even better because they got more stuff for energy."

My mother slept in the back seat. I slept in the front because I was smaller and could lie under the steering wheel. Late that night, I heard my mother open the car door. I found her sitting on her blanket leaning against the bumper of the car.

"You see all those stars," she said. "When I was a little girl, my grandmother used to take me and my sisters out on the prairies and tell us stories about all the stars."

"Do you think Mel is going to bring us any hamburgers?"

"Every one of those stars has a story. You see that bunch of stars over there that look like a fish?"

"He didn't say no."

"Coyote went fishing, one day. That's how it all started." We sat out under the stars that night, and my mother told me all sorts of stories. She was serious about it, too. She'd tell them slow, repeating parts as she went, as if she expected me to remember each one.

Early the next morning, the television vans began to arrive, and guys in suits and women in dresses came trotting over to us, dragging microphones and cameras and lights behind them. One of the vans had a table set up with orange juice and sandwiches and fruit. It was for the crew, but when I told them we hadn't eaten for a while, a really skinny blonde woman told us we could eat as much as we wanted.

They mostly talked to my mother. Every so often one of the reporters would come over and ask me questions about how it felt to be an Indian without a country. I told them we had a nice house on the reserve and that my cousins had a couple of horses we rode when we went fishing. Some of the television people went over to the American border, and then they went to the Canadian border.

Around noon, a good-looking guy in a dark blue suit and an orange tie with little ducks on it drove up in a fancy car. He talked to my mother for a while, and, after they were done talking, my mother called me over, and we got into our car. Just as my mother started the engine, Mel came over and gave us a bag of peanut brittle and told us that justice was a damn hard thing to get, but that we shouldn't give up.

I would have preferred lemon drops, but it was nice of Mel anyway.

"Where we going now?"

"Going to visit Laetitia."

The guard who came out to our car was all smiles. The television lights were so bright they hurt my eyes, and, if you tried to look through the windshield in certain directions, you couldn't see a thing.

"Morning ma'am."

"Good morning."

"Where you heading?"

"Salt Lake City."

"Purpose of your visit?"

"Visit my daughter."

"Any tobacco, liquor, or firearms?"

"Don't smoke."

"Any plants or fruit?"

"Not any more."

"Citizenship?"

"Blackfoot."

The guard rocked back on his heels and jammed his thumbs into his gun belt. "Thank you," he said, his fingers patting the butt of the revolver. "Have a pleasant trip."

My mother rolled the car forward, and the television people had to scramble out of the way. They ran alongside the car as we pulled away from the border, and, when they couldn't run any farther, they stood in the middle of the highway and waved and waved and waved.

We got to Salt Lake City the next day. Laetitia was happy to see us, and, that first night, she took us out to a restaurant that made really good soups. The list of pies took up a whole page. I had cherry. Mom had chocolate. Laetitia said that she saw us on television the night before, and, during the meal, she had us tell her the story over and over again.

Laetitia took us everywhere. We went to a fancy ski resort. We went to the temple. We got to go shopping in a couple of large malls, but they weren't as large as the one in Edmonton, and Mom said so.

After a week or so, I got bored and wasn't at all sad when my mother said we should be heading back home. Laetitia wanted us to stay longer, but Mom said no, that she had things to do back home and that, next time, Laetitia should come up and visit. Laetitia said she was thinking about moving back, and Mom told her to do as she pleased, and Laetitia said that she would.

On the way home, we stopped at the duty-free shop and my mother gave Mel a green hat that said "Salt Lake" across the front. Mel was a funny guy. He took the hat and blew his nose and told my mother that she was an inspiration to us all. He gave us some more peanut brittle and came out into the parking lot and waved at us all the way to the Canadian border.

It was almost evening when we left Coutts. I watched the border through the rear window until all you could see were the tops of the flagpoles and the blue water tower, and then they rolled over a hill and disappeared.

Mermaids

Richard Van Camp

Come flying out of the Range Hotel. Elbow's busted. Bleeding through my sock. Gotta find those sisters. Right rump is sore. Took the fall so I wouldn't go through the TV. Yellowknife. I hate this town. Cabees everywhere. The little girl I saw waiting earlier is still there. Waiting. Still waiting. For who? Her folks? She's got those yellow gumboots on. Christ, she's gotta be cold. It's late. What time is it? Gotta make that bus. I feel my blood drain and pool in my shoe. I head towards her. Her face is filthy. She's shivering. I gotta make that bus.

"You're bleeding," she says.

I lean hard against a parking meter. "You should be inside."

"I can stay out late as I want," she insists.

My throat. Everything starts spinning. My mother was cursed. I swallow blood. The day she bore me. I stare at the little girl and I am faint with envy of the dead. "Did I ever tell you why God killed the mermaids?"

That's when I black out.

When I come to, I'm in an apartment. Awful little apartment. Black velvet paintings on the wall. Sticky beer on the kitchen floor. Something sticky all over me. I look. Band-Aids. I got Barbie Band-Aids on my arms and hands. All over my throat and face. There's a party next door. We hear it. I'm sitting down with my sock off. Did she drag me here? She comes around the corner holding something.

"What do you got there?"

"My last Band-Aid," she says, "for your foot."

I look down. The skin on the back of my foot is torn absolutely off. It's stopped bleeding. Lint and hair on my pink wound.

"Okay," I say.

She rolls the Band-Aid on while I wiggle my toes. "Don't pick it," she says.

I look around. I'm sitting on urea foam furniture. Christ, these people.

Don't they know anything?

"Don't pick it," she warns. "Don't pick it. Don't pick it."

"Where's your mom?"

"Working."

"Yeah right," I say. "This late?"

She crosses her arms. "My mom's working."

"Okay, kid, okay. You're the boss. Does your mom have any smokes around here, or what?"

Shakes her head. How old is she?

"Why did God kill the mermaids?"

"Come on," I say. "You don't want to know why God killed them."

"Sure I do," she says. Before I know it, she sits on my knee. I think I chipped the blade of my elbow off. I can't seem to move it. Legs are tightening up too. Who would have guessed I could kick them so far forward?

"How old are you?" I ask.

"Nine," she says.

My meds. Good thing I take my meds. I can miss two meals and never feel it cuz I take my meds.

"What happened to your arms?" she asks.

My tattoos. She's covered my tattoos with Barbie Band-Aids. I smoldered them off with a car lighter after Sfen died. They were home-grown crosses Sfen gimme, one on each arm. "Accident," I say. "What's your name?"

"Stephanie. What's yours?"

"You never heard of me?"

She shakes her head.

"You sure?" I look around. "My name is Torchy."

"That's not your name," she says.

"Sure it is."

"What's your real name?"

I look around again. No one here but us. "Hazel," I say. "But I hate that name. Call me Torchy."

"Why do they call you Torchy?"

"You don't want to know."

Her eyes light up. "Sure I do."

34

"Because I like to burn things down," I say.

"Why?"

"I got a gene variant."

"A what?"

"A cocaine gland in my brain. It spills sometimes."

She frowns. "Don't lie."

"Hey. How does God clean?"

"With his hands."

"No. He cleans with fire. And I would rather unleash fire than have fire unleash me."

She doesn't get it. She doesn't even hear me. She pouts her lips. "But firebugs pee their bed."

"What?"

"My daddy told me firebugs pee their bed."

I laugh for the first time in months. "Where's your old man?"

She doesn't answer. Looks down. I shoulda known better.

"Why did God kill the mermaids, Torchy?"

"God killed the mermaids," I say. "He did, you know."

She looks at me with a filthy face. Rests her little head on my bony shoulder. "But why?"

Jesus, this kid trusts me. Doesn't she know who I am? Eleven o'clock at night. Her folks are drinkin' and she's here with me. Okay. She saved me so maybe I owe her. I need time. Need to power up. It's eleven now. I gotta make that midnight bus.

"Well," I say, "this is a story. It's not an old time story. It's not a 'Once upon a Time' story. It's a Torchy story and, Christ, I wish your mom had a smoke around here. I can feel my brain swelling."

"Torchy —"

"Okay. Okay. The best I can figure is when sailors saw the mermaids, they leapt from their boats and swam to them. They forgot about their houses, their mortgages, their ol' ladies, they forgot about all that. They saw such beautiful women. They just wanted to be with them. And if they died swimming across, they died with glory in their eyes. Then they saw the mermen. While they were swimming. These mermen were so beautiful they fell in love with them, too. They became bi-sexual."

I look at the little girl for her reaction. She's listening but she's got sleepy eyes.

"You know what that means?" She shakes her head. "That means you love everyone and everything around you. You love men. You love women. You love puppies and you love Country and Western music. You just love everything. And everyone. The mermaids and mermen were so beautiful, the humans wanted to stay there forever until they died. They carved temples out of Chinese jade for them, so the mermaids and mermen could sit on altars. The mermen would have to remind the humans to eat. Humans were so in love they forgot to eat. Like the bison when they're rutting. They forget to eat, eh? They just wanted love."

I look. She's almost asleep. "God killed the mermaids because they were more beautiful than God. Humans worshipped mermaids and mermen. Humans forgot about God and anytime humans forget about God He reminds them that He's still there. That's why he brought AIDS. Because we forgot."

I flex my fingers. Make a fist. Oh, I'm gonna feel this all tomorrow. I lean back in the chair. I hope my throat doesn't close. I hold Stephanie close. I hold her. I hold her. She's still got those gumboots on. I hug her and hold her close.

"Where do fish sleep?" she asks suddenly.

"I thought you were sleeping. What?"

"Where do fish sleep?"

"I don't know."

She smiles. "On river beds, silly."

"Oh," I say. Then we burst out laughing.

She studies me deep. "Are you a bad man, Torchy?"

I think about this long and hard. "Am I a bad man?" I ask. "I'm not a bad man. I just leave for a while and let the bad man in."

I think of another logo me and Sfen could have done if he would have met this little girl. It would say, LAUGHTER IS THE BEST MEDICINE and under it we could have little kid's handwriting that says: AND HUGS HELP TOO.

They used to call my brother "the idea man." He was a logo artist by trade, but I couldn't think about that. I lift Stephanie and place her on the sofa.

Where's Stephanie's mom? Doesn't she know guys worse than me walked the streets? Some guys right now would be pullin' their junk lookin' at her.

I call Sfen. I let his phone ring a full five minutes just to listen to it ring. Why hasn't it been disconnected? There's a life lived between every ring. A life lived. How much money do I got left? Four hundreds. There's a red crayon. Good. I take it and write with on each bill, "My mother was cursed the day she bore me. I am faint with envy of the dead."

I look out the window to the Yellowknife sky. I love how clouds here fold themselves and burn for sunsets. I pray, I guess, in my own way. Bless these bills, someone. May each of these bills burn to sunlight. May each of these bills change lives forever, for good.

How'm I gonna explain this to Snowbird? The old man who blessed my hands and warned me, "Grandson," he said, "make sure you drop some tobacco when you get to Yellowknife. Say your name out loud after you land so your soul can catch up with you and don't forget to wash your hands after you win."

It was only yesterday when I worked up the courage to go see him.

"Old man?" I called as I walked into his porch.

"A-mi-nay?" he asked. "Who's there?"

"Maybe I'm your long lost grandson, and maybe I want to make my long lost grandpa rich."

The medicine man called Snowbird studied me with glassy, filmy eyes. It looked like someone had emptied an egg into each of his eyes. We were quiet for a bit. I recognized the music on the radio. It was Van Morrison's "Sometimes I feel like a motherless child." It was a hurtin' song so we listened hard.

He opened the door of his wood stove with a piece of fresh kindling, and popped a large spruce in before closing the door with the same stick. He waved the glowing stick around in the air and we could see and smell its beautiful sweet smoke.

"I remember you when you were this high," he lifted his brown hand to his knee. "Hey-ya-hay!" the old man smiled, "I better put on some tea so me and my long lost grandson can catch up. Also, we should pray now that we have found each other after all these years."

Snowbird must have been the loneliest man in the world, the way he moved. He pulled out a pouch of Drum and opened his wood stove. He threw in a pinch of tobacco and began to pray in Dogrib. I was disgusted with how lonely he was. He was starving for someone to talk to. I watched him pray and didn't understand a word. He then switched to English: "...and this is for my adopted grandson," he said. Then he handed the pouch to me. "Now you, Grandson."

I pinched some tobacco and pulled it out. "For everyone with AIDS," I said.

"Ho," he said.

I threw the tobacco to the naked fire. It smelled sweet.

"For my brother Sfen."

"Ho."

I was just about to cross myself, but suddenly remembered: "For all my enemies."

"Ho!" he said really loud. Maybe I was praying for us both.

"I'm sorry to hear, Grandpa," I said, "that your wife died."

"Yes yes," he answered sadly, "but that is God's plan. Not ours. It's up to the boss upstairs." He pointed with the piece of kindling to the ceiling. "Jesus was a medicine man."

"Here are the signs," he said as he sucked on his pipe. "There are three wolves running outside of town. Three wolves. One is white. One is gray. One is black. Wolves are how the Creator moves over the snow."

I thought of lepers and tornadoes touching down.

He was quiet for a while before he said, "There is talk of a midnight burial outside of town, by the lake."

I cleared my throat but couldn't speak. Don't ask about my brother, I was thinking. Don't you dare ask about my brother.

He waited a long, long time before saying with a soft voice, "That's all right, Grandson. We do what we have to, don't we?"

I nodded, waited for the tears to stop burning my eyes. How did he know? I waited, nodded again, looked away. How did he know? He poured us some tea and turned the radio off.

"Why have you come here, Grandson?"

I took a big breath. "I want the jackpot in tomorrow's Bingo in Yellowknife. Eighty grand cash. I'll give you half if you bless my hands with your medicine."

He thought about it. Nodded. "Come visit your grandpa tomorrow before you leave," he said.

Great! "But I have to get on the plane. Will it last until Yellowknife?"

"Yes. Just don't touch any cards or Bingo dabbers until you get to the game you want to win."

"What if we have to share the pot with someone in Y.K.?"

"You won't."

I waited. "What will you do with your half, old man?"

He was quiet for even longer. It was like he was listening to the fire and the words of the song and each instrument in the band and maybe the thoughts of each band player and mister Van. It was as if he realized again how pitiful he was hugging such loneliness every day. "Do you know what I wish?" he asked. "I wish someone were to visit me and read to me the Bible. It is such a beautiful song sung with so many voices. I could make tea and we could talk after. That's what I wish, Grandson."

I stood up. Me? He was talking about me.

"I don't want money," he continued. "You're young. You keep it. But please remember your Grandpa."

A medicine man saying please to me. I couldn't believe it. He held out his small, brittle hand. I took it. It was almost like his fingers were made with the same tiny hollow bones in sparrow wings.

"Is there a woman in your life, Grandson? Where are all my grandchildren?"

I remembered me and Sfen sneaking out to the highway at night to hunt ptarmigan sitting high in the poplars. "There's no such thing as '90s love," I said and pushed away. "The earth is burning, Grandpa."

"Why do you talk like this?"

I looked into his blind eyes. "It's gonna take hell for me to find another heart that beats like mine."

He nodded. Didn't know what the hell I was talking about.

"I have to go, Grandpa."

"Come visit me tomorrow," he said. "I'll bless your hands."

I coughed I would. "Grandpa," I said. "Can I ask you a question?"

"That's what grandpas are for."

"Why don't you cure yourself? Your eyes, I mean."

He worked his little tight lips around his fake teeth. "I would have to kill a man and take his eyes," he said. "Then where would I be? I just have to tap my cane and children take me where I wish to go. If I could see, they would not help me any more. I am already in heaven, Grandson. You were the one who could smell the fireweed roots, weren't you?"

That's right! I had forgotten. I remembered taking the old man's cane and leading him to the Bay when I was a child.

"What do you smell, Grandson?" he would ask.

"Fire," I'd answer. "I smell fire."

He would chuckle deep into his chest. I could smell fire even when I was a little boy, and I could smell cancer in trees. So how did I end up bloody in Yellowknife with blessed hands? I won the Bingo game, all right, just like the old man said I would. I had eighty thousand dollars cash in two duffel bags. I should have put it in storage, but I ended up taking a taxi right to the top of the Gold Range. I figured the old man's medicine could win me more. It did. I won every hand I played: Blackjack, Poker. I got the Gook who ran the place to bring me some ginger pork and rice. And then I saw the hookers, two Gook sisters who wanted me, so I bought a room, but I forgot to wash my hands.

I woke up choking after throwing fire into both twins. I was being choked. I looked for someone to kill. No one. There was no one I could see, then I realized they were my own hands choking off my windpipe. The twins shot up screaming. My own hands were killing me. I couldn't breathe. I was gagging so I charged to the bathroom. I knew what was happening. The old man's medicine ran out and turned sour. I sat down and pulled my legs back and kicked my arms loose. That's when I saw them. I had claws instead of hands. The devil's claws were on me. The same hands that won me eighty grand were digging through my throat. But I got the tub going. I got it going and I put those claws under the bloody water for a long time until they turned back to my hands. When I went back to the room, the twins had vanished with all my money.

I remembered the night Sfen told me everything. We were at the Lake. It was such a pretty night for sin. We were relaxing after kicking in the door and looting the Warden's house. Sfen knew the Warden was in the city with his ol' lady. And just like the song, there was a smoke on the water. There were parties rocking hard across the lake. Sitting around our fire, counting stars, trying to make out the voices, we strained to hear what they were talking about.

"This is my favorite place in the whole world, brother," he said.

I thought about it. "Mine too, I guess."

We could hear ducks laugh with wooden throats somewhere not too far away. A few mallards whistled by overhead. There was a breeze then, the first breeze of summer. It was cool and it whispered through the hair on our arms. We shared the Warden's smokes, passed the Warden's bottle. That's when Sfen told me everything.

But I had known a long time ago. The way his skull sucked his face in. The night sweats that drenched his mattress.

I should have asked the old man if he had medicine for AIDS. What animal would know which part of itself to give? The caribou? I heard the cure for cancer is in the root of a bear's tongue. But which part, and which cancer? There are so many now.

"What am I gonna do, Torch?" Sfen asked. He had lost so much weight the last year. He couldn't stop his hands from shaking and he wiped his tears away with his sleeve. "It's getting worse every day. I can't take it anymore and I don't want to take it anymore."

I tried so hard to think of the perfect answer and it suddenly hit me we were sharing the same bottle and the same cigarette. Could you get AIDS from that?

"What would a wolf do?" I asked Sfen.

"That isn't the question," Sfen said. "What would a sick wolf do? I have AIDS, Torchy. I'm dying. I ran outta my pills yesterday and I ain't going to the drug store in town. If anyone finds out, Torch, we're both dead and you know it. We ain't exactly town heroes."

"You're out of meds? Sfen, you need those. What are we doing here then? Christ, we should make a run to the city and get some more."

I started shaking. Something was up. That's when he said, "You know,

Torch, I been thinking. All my furniture is stuffed with that urea foam. You told me once it releases cyanide gas when it burns."

I stood up and yelled, "What are you talking like this for!?"

"I'd sit up when I heard the fire alarm," he continued. "You'd have to do it when I was asleep. I'd sit up and breathe two lungs full. It'd be painless, wouldn't it? You'd do that for me wouldn't you?"

"No!" I said. "Never! Sfen don't talk like that!" And that's when I ran. I ran all the way up the road as far as I could. I ran until I puked. I was thinking this wasn't happening. I kept waiting for someone to tell me this wasn't real. I was thinking until I couldn't think any more and that's when I heard the shot.

The Warden's gun.

The one we found under the bed. The one I was gonna take back to town and stash.

On the beach. There was blood everywhere when I found him. My brother's eyes were still open. I never seen blood so red. The Warden's rosary braided through his fingers. Sfen's eyes wide open. Looking at the lake. I never seen blood so red.

The party didn't even stop across the lake. People just hooted and cheered when they heard the shot.

Now Sfen is where the fish sleep. At the lake, by the river bed. My brother who loved mermen.

"Torchy? Torchy!" Stephanie is shaking me. "Torchy? You were having a nightmare."

I look around, covered in sweat. "I was?"

"You were calling for Sfen. Who's Sfen?"

I look down. "My brother."

"Where is he? Is that who you were looking for?"

"Yeah," I wipe my sleeve across my eyes, "but he's gone."

"Just like my daddy's gone," she says. "My mom says he was fast. Faster than the wind. He froze to death, she says. Maybe the wind caught him." She looks at me and says, "I'll be your sister, Torchy, if you'll be my brother."

I can feel it build. I don't want to scare her so I move fast and I pick her up. I hug her and I start to cry. I have to keep it quiet but I can't stop.

"Take me with you, Torchy," she says. "I don't want to stay here anymore. I'm scared all the time. I'll wash floors, I'll cook, I'll clean..."

I thought of the old man and I looked at my hands. "Do you want to come with me? To where I live?"

She looked around. "What about my mom?"

"We'll call your mom when things get better, okay? There's a bus leaving in half an hour to Simmer. There's an old man I want you to meet — my grandpa. He really wants to meet you."

She scratched her head and smiled. "He does?"

"Yeah," I said. "He does. Can you read?"

She nodded. "Let's go, Torchy. Let's go to your home."

I remembered Sfen, when we were kids. One of my mom's boyfriends felt guilty, I guess, for beating on all of us. He took us to the lake after for a picnic of chips and beer. He also bought one pair of flippers for me and Sfen.

Mom needed shades to hide the love he put on her. "You're gonna have to learn to share," she called weakly as we ran from the car. "You two are brothers and brothers share."

"It's okay, Torchy," Sfen whispered. "Don't look at him."

Sfen's left eye was swollen shut. He had to help me with mine because my arms were so sore. I got the right flipper because I had smaller feet. He took the left, though it was too tight for him. We held hands and ran to the water. The same lake I buried him beside. We ran together, my big brother and me, never letting go, laughing, free...

American Indian

United States of
America

The Farm

Sherman Alexie

1. Jonah

All of us, the Indians, know exactly where we were
when scientists announced that they had found the cure

for cancer. I was eating lunch in the Tribal Cafe
for the third time that week and was only halfway

through my fry bread when the national news broke
into the local news: a white man in a lab coat

stood at a podium porcupined with microphones
and quietly spoke. "We have found that the bone

marrow of Indians, synthesized with a few trace
elements, forms a powerful antiviral agent named

Steptoe 123. This agent, when taken orally, will
stop the metastatic growth of tumors and kill

cancer cells. Steptoe 123 has been 95% effective
in ten years of research under the direction

of Dr. Miles Steptoe at the Center for Disease
Control. We have prepared a detailed press release

which will give you more information on Steptoe
123, Dr. Steptoe, and all that you need to know

at this time. The President, with a clear vision
of the future of Steptoe 123, has made a decision.

Therefore, under the authority of Executive Order
1492, we have closed all of the reservation borders

within the United States and will keep them closed
to any and all unauthorized traffic until further notice."

Silence. Then I turned to Charlie the Cook, who was really
the dishwasher. "Jonah," he asked me. "Is it real?"

"It's real," I said. Charlie looked at me, looked
at Agnes the Waitress, who was really the cook.

"Why is it real?" asked Charlie, but it was too late
for a history lesson. We all needed to escape

before the borders were completely shut down.
"We've got to go," I said. "We've got to go now."

So Agnes, Charlie, and I jumped into my old car
and prayed it would save us like that famous ark

but we didn't even make it past
Cold Springs before we heard the first dissonant

music: the helicopters played ragtime as they fell
from Heaven, as one descended on us with propeller

blades that broke our hearts and windshield.
I drove the car off the road and into a field

where everything stopped
as Sam the Indian, who

was really white, suddenly stepped onto the road
with his hands out, palms open, just inches below

that helicopter, as Charlie asked, "Where did he
come from?" I just remember Sam was whittled

to bone as the helicopter dropped down onto him.
(Did you know you can play a gospel hymn

on a flute carved from human bone? I heard
the hymn once, in a dream, but have since learned

to play it on a hollow femur.) The soldiers came
for us then, dragged us from the car, asked for our names

and tribal affiliations, demanded to know if the guy
killed under the helicopter was Indian or white.

"He was white," I said. "Fully white?" a soldier asked
and I told him that Sam the Indian might be the last

fully good white man in America. "The dead guy ain't Feeder
or Breeder," shouted the soldier. Sam wasn't needed

because the scientists couldn't use his bone marrow
so the soldiers left Sam's body to the crows and sparrows.

"What am I?" I asked the soldier as he tied my hands behind
my back with soft cotton twine, but he did not reply.

"What am I?" I asked the soldier as they carried
me to the helicopter. "Are you single or married?"

asked a soldier. "I'm a bag of bones," I said.
"Do you have any children," the soldier asked again

and again, but I kept telling him I was all alone
in this new world, that I was just a bag of bones.

2. Sam the Indian

When the blades fell upon me
I was closer to being Indian than I had ever been before.
When the blades fell upon me
I was closer to being Indian than I had ever been before.
When the blades fell upon me
I was closer to being Indian than I had ever been before.
When the blades fell upon me
I was closer to being Indian than I had ever been before.
When the blades fell upon me
I was closer to being Indian than I had ever been before.
When the blades fell upon me
I was closer to being Indian than I had ever been before.
When the blades fell upon me
I was closer to being Indian than I had ever been before.

3. Charlie the Cook

After we were captured by the soldiers, they took all of the Indians to a
place called the Farm. My history became their history. They took notes.
They tattooed my forehead with a B for Breeder, because I was young and
pure-blood. They keep the Breeder men and women together. In each cell,

there are five women and one man. We are rotated often, never allowed to develop relationships. We are not allowed to talk. We are never in the same cell with a member of the same tribe. Bright lights wake us at 6 a.m. We eat breakfast only after we procreate. I'm supposed to have sex with five Indian women a day. I have fathered dozens of children since this all started. Half of my children became Breeders and stayed at the Farm, while the other half became Feeders and were sent to the Kitchen. The Feeders have it much worse than the Breeders. The Feeders have their marrow taken from them. They are hooked up to machines that suck it out. Sometimes they survive. Sometimes they die. It happens to children, too. There is no age limit. When they need the marrow, they take it. There's constant demand. Each cancer patient needs a year's worth of Steptoe 123. Late at night, in the cell, I reach my hand out into the dark and I feel another hand reaching out for mine. I cannot see who I touch. We cannot speak. But we hold each other's hands lightly, ready to release our grips at any moment.

4. Agnes the Waitress

When the Indian men come to me
I try to smile.

I lift my tunic
and part my legs

with as much honor
as I can manage.

I try to love the Indian men
who are forced to enter me.

It would be easy to hate them.
Some women do.

Some women refuse
to acknowledge the man's body.

Some women close their eyes
and imagine a new childhood.

Some women weep constantly.
They don't last long.

But I hold the men close
and kiss their necks.

That always surprises them.
They stare at me

and I wonder if
I am beautiful.

I have forgotten
what that means.

I cannot tell the difference
between a beautiful man

and an ugly man
because it makes no difference.

We do not have the luxury
of such a decision.

We are Indian
and that is all that matters

though it is rumored
that white guards sneak

into bed with Indian women.
I have heard the rustling

of blankets late at night
when Indian women crawled

into bed with Indian women.
An Indian woman once kissed me

and I felt her hands on my breasts.
I reached for her, too

but the guard rushed in
and took her away.

I never saw her again.
I dream about her

though I cannot tell you
if she was beautiful.

I want to believe
my babies are beautiful

though I have learned to let them go.
I give birth.

I heal.
I am pregnant again.

Pregnancy is the good time.
Pregnant women share a cell.

We eat well.
We are not touched.

We are allowed to speak
to the body inside our own

and pretend it is our mother,
father, sister, and brother.

5. Charlie the Cook

We have developed a highly complex and subtle sign language. Through slight gestures, such as brushing the hair from our faces, we can talk about the past. The volume of a cough can change the tense of a sentence. A woman can sit up in bed, scratch her cheek, stand quickly, shuffle across the room to a water fountain, take a big drink, swallow loudly, and we'd all know she was telling a joke. Indians always find a way to laugh, though each of us laughs in a different way. I laugh by crossing my arms. I cry by tapping my left foot against the floor.

6. Agnes the Waitress

I try to find the soldiers beneath their masks.
I try to find the doctors behind their sorrow.

The white people never thought to ask
if we would voluntarily donate the marrow.

7. Jonah

We've been planning the revolution for years.
We have weapons and white friends, but I fear

Indians have forgotten how to survive.
It's a complicated song and dance. Late at night

we practice. We pound invisible drums. We sing
with our mouths closed. Silence is the thing

we must learn to fear. This is the plan.
One night, we will slip from our beds and stand

together. We will stamp our feet in unison
and sing the same song loudly with strong lungs

and hearts. We will sing the old songs.
Cousins, this is not where we belong.

Way, ya, hi, yo. Way, ya, hi, yo.
Way, ya, hi, yo. Way, ya, hi, yo.

Cousins, remember how we sang and danced back then.
During the revolution, we will find our music again.

8. Sam the Indian

When I fell into Heaven
I was closer to being Indian than I had ever been before.
When I fell into Heaven
I was closer to being Indian than I had ever been before.

When I fell into Heaven
I was closer to being Indian than I had ever been before.
When I fell into Heaven
I was closer to being Indian than I had ever been before.
When I fell into Heaven
I was closer to being Indian than I had ever been before.
When I fell into Heaven
I was closer to being Indian than I had ever been before.
When I fell into Heaven
I was closer to being Indian than I had ever been before.
When I fell into Heaven
I was closer to being Indian than I had ever been before.
When I fell into Heaven
I was closer to being Indian than I had ever been before.

9. Charlie the Cook

I have not seen a black man in years. Not a black woman. Not a Mexican man, though their blood is often mixed with Indians, too. I have not seen another Indian man. I have seen only white men and Indian women. There are rumors. The Indian women have refused to procreate, and instead, they are killing the Indian men. It would be easy. In each cell, five women to each man. There are rumors. Indian men are becoming sterile. We have fathered too many children. There are rumors. The revolution is about to begin. Indians will rise against our jailers. We will never touch each other again. We will allow ourselves to die as a people, rather than live as we do now. There are rumors. A large army of sympathetic outsiders, white, black, brown, and yellow, are preparing to storm the Farm. They will free us. There are rumors. All of the cancer is gone. It has been completely destroyed. Our jailers will soon open the doors and let us free. They will give us medals of honor as we leave.

Fancy Dog Contest

Kimberly Blaeser

The dog stories started again last October in the Corner Store. I was working after school, just like I had been doing since I was ten. It's my Auntie's store and she sells most everything the folks in Pudge Lakes want that they don't go to town for. The Post Office is right in there, too, and Auntie has a gas pump outside. So it's a pretty busy place. Weekends and most evenings she has coffee made for those who want to sit and visit which is just about everybody who comes in. You know how it is. The talk is free and that makes up for the prices on everything else.

Well that evening there was a table full of leechers that should have been out checking their traps, but once Ronny Two Mink's dog wandered in and started the stories, wasn't anyone there going to leave. That's what I like about working for Auntie Todd — you can hear all kinds of village news and old time tales, too, without anybody paying you a bit of notice. I was unpacking canned goods, wiping off their lids, and putting them away, practicing my whistle while I did it. Maybe that's what brought that fat Martha Beth into the store or maybe she just followed someone in because she liked the smell of them.

Anyway, in she came and right away she started making the rounds at the leech table, offering to shake hands. She went from one guy to the next, waiting by their chair, pawing up and down. All the guys shook just polite as you please. And then Martha Beth started her tricks. She puts on quite an act. You ought to come see. Sits up to beg, prances across the floor, and rolls over and over. She's really pretty good at it, but nowadays sometimes old age and her belly get in the way. Still she keeps it up until someone feeds her. So that bearded guy Truck yelled to me to bring them some beef jerky and that's what Martha Beth carried off.

Then they started explaining to the new boy from the city — everyone likes to show off like that with city folks. I heard this guy called Ringworm and

Raymond so I don't know what name he's gonna end up with, but he was a good listener. "Martha's one of the new *educated* reservation dogs," one of the leechers told him and they all laughed, because they knew good stories were coming. I knew it, too, and I was anxious. I wanted to hear about the Bush brothers. But, of course, it starts with the dogs.

Outsiders have a hard time understanding the way Indians are with their dogs, just like they are always puzzled about Indians and their kids. Maybe in some ways the two patterns are alike. Dogs in Indian communities are lavished one minute and kicked under the table the next. And children, well, they're prized beyond almost any material thing, but then they have the air knocked out of them when they least expect it. I don't mean physically necessarily, although that's true, too, sometimes. I mean the way you feel when something happens that suddenly makes you go limp with loss. My Uncle William once told me about a drunk hunter who shot his own dog when it got beat out in retrieving. "I can still see the betrayal in the eyes of that animal as it looked at the barrel," he said. "It turned away and went dead before that fool even pulled the trigger." Well I've seen plenty children wearing that look, and with reason enough.

But it's not the alcohol cruelty that makes reservations different from any other place, it's the strange loyalties. And the way they flow back and forth between children and parents, animals and humans. I don't know if you can understand, but it's like what happened between my Grandma and her old dog Larky. Grandma and that dog had been together through two moves and ten kids. Larky didn't have a fancy life. She lived under the house, protected in winter by bales of hay piled around the skirting. And she survived mostly on scraps and table slop. I don't even remember Grandma spending much time with Larky, just a quick scratch on her way to the woodpile or a pat while shucking corn. But they were friends. I knew that because Grandma could set Larky's tail to wagging more than anyone and Larky always started Grandma on a mumbling conversation. Well that dog was old and beginning to suffer, her hind legs almost too weak to hold her up. My Grandma finally told one of her boys to build a box and ready his gun. But the next morning they found Larky had just died. You see, that's what those two would do for one another.

And it's because Indians are loyal to their dogs in that way and their dogs are loyal to them even if it means sharing their poverty, that the dog population is always high around the village. And just like extra relatives are found in almost every house in the village, extra dogs seemed to attach themselves to every family, too. Used to be you couldn't walk to the outhouse around here without three or four dogs starting to bark. Wasn't anybody getting a full night's sleep and they were always scaring someone. My mom lost more than one pail of hazelnuts when someone's dog had a bark too close to her. Could be somebody complained. But more than likely the federal health people just showed up by themselves. My Uncle Timberwolf used to say the federal agents were like poison ivy, popping up every year, always right in your path, and good at starting an itch that would keep spreading until everyone was uncomfortable whether they were scratching or watching.

Anyway some officials started saying the mongrels were a nuisance and a hazard, carried diseases, and were dangerous. So they did what the government does best and started a program. They wanted all the dogs to get shots and licenses. But nobody was going to claim two or three animals when it meant it was gonna cost fifteen dollars a head. Far as I know there isn't a single licensed dog in the village yet. But they did get their shots. A big paddy wagon came in every weekend for a month and lots of young vet students chased around catching as many animals as they could, giving them shots, and tagging them. Sinner Jacob used to charge people five cents apiece to set up their lawn chairs in his yard and watch. He says he's got lots of good tales stored up from those days, but so far I haven't heard him telling them. Maybe he's gonna charge for stories, too. Anyway, those student veterinarians stopped coming after ticks progressed to grey and ready-to-pop.

Everything was quiet for awhile, except for the dogs kept barking. Then after a year or two some agency started *Phase Two*. But this time they must have asked around on how to get people to go along with it. So they put up posters — *Dog Training Classes. Learn to be in command*. They sponsored a contest that offered big prize money: *Win five hundred dollars for first place, two hundred for second, and one hundred for third!* They also started having food at training meetings, and somehow they got the two Bush brothers to enter their dogs. Those guys hadn't talked to one another for eighteen years and people started coming to the community center just to see what would happen with them both there at the same time. But the teacher didn't let you just hang around unless you brought a dog. So pretty soon almost all the dogs were being claimed. Sometimes if someone didn't have anything better to do and wanted to eat and gossip they would borrow a relative's dog for the night. And so the fancy dog contest replaced cribbage and friendship cakes the year I turned eight.

The first sign of craziness came after those people training dogs were told they had to have collars and leashes. It was almost like pow-wow time around here, with grandmas, aunties and uncles all costuming the kids. A dog might have a few ribs showing, but you can bet it was going to wear one fine collar. No one was satisfied with a plain old Ben Franklin variety. You ain't never seen such fancy hunks of leather. Missus Manypoint made up the prettiest little deerskin collar edged with large blue trade beads for her Samantha Wolfe. Old Sid Cottonwood had his mum lazystitch an eighteen-inch collar and the whole length of the leash for his labrador. And just like Sid, all the folks started naming the breeds of their dogs or the breeds they imagined them to be in order to register them. Jim "Dandy" Trautner, who likes to call himself "The Fisherman", linked together a bunch of red spinners to make a collar for his *malamute* (which he used to just call a sled dog). English setter, blue dane, springer/poodle cross, terrier/fox mixed blood. Turned into another whole kind of contest I guess you could say, but one Indian people had lots of practice at anyways — bloodlines, stories, and invented identities.

Course it didn't stop there. One week after the dogs were issued numbers they started showing up in fancy outfits. Frank Rabbit's second wife Linda from Pine Ridge brought her husky in wearing sled boots decorated plains style. They were better than most moccasins. The story goes she had to carry that dog in because he couldn't get used to anything on his feet and kept trying to find a way to walk without stepping down on the leather. He kept at least one foot off the floor all the time, shaking his paws, walking on his two hind legs and then on the front ones like he was a circus poodle. Finally the poor critter just rolled over on his back and froze. Linda was sure put out at that dog which people started calling Possum after it stiffened itself out just like it was dead. And they say that dog ain't never walked the same since. I see him sometimes kind of slinking around, his tail drooping, stopping every step or two to hold up a paw like he has a thorn in it. Some things stay with you, I guess, for good or bad.

Well maybe Possum's getup didn't work out too well, but some of them dogs took to the fancying up like princes and princesses. Fat Martha Beth here had a little pendleton coat with a mink collar and Jimmy Sledge's terrier-cross Sun Dog had something like a grass dance outfit in rainbow colors. Both of them went round those training circles with their little black noses and stubby tails held real high. Beads, feathers, tobacco cans, bones, skins — there's nothing you've seen stitched into a dance outfit that didn't end up on somebody's dog.

Of course, everyone watched the Bush brothers. But at first it seemed they weren't going to go to any trouble costuming their dogs. Folks call the brothers "Rusty" and "Dollar", the names they got about the same time their argument started. It was because of what the one brother did to the other one's pickup when they were just out of the service — drove it into Pickerel Lake one night. He did go through the trouble of towing it out, but then he just left it in the woods to rust. And he convinced his big brother that he had lost the truck himself in a bet with a Roy Laker. It was half a year before the truth got out. Meanwhile the second Bush bought a swanky blue pickup that he kept real clean and started using it to take his brother's girl to town. He got his name because he was always saying his truck was as shiny as a silver dollar. Until the truck thing, the brothers had always hung together. Story is Rusty washed and dressed Dollar from the time their mum passed on. Later they were the only two Indians in their army platoon, so they had to keep each other remembering and believing they'd come home. I've seen pictures of them back then. In their uniforms you could hardly tell them apart, one standing like a reflection of the other. *Like two peas in a pod* my mom used to say. She says they still are and that's what made them so mad at one another. Course Rusty began to look his six years older once he started to carry his mad with him so long and now no one would mistake him for his slick-tongued brother.

Well anyway when they came to the second meeting their dogs had the plainest training collars of the whole bunch and Rusty had just an ordinary piece of clothesline rope instead of a real leash. Folks were kind of disappointed about that.

The Bush dogs had come from the same litter, but Dollar called his Spike a wolfhound and Rusty called Spitfire a borzoi. Neither one looked like those Irish or Russian dogs in the World Book Encyclopedia except for being long-legged and pretty shaggy. At least at the beginning of the contest that's how they looked. Third meeting, Dollar brings in Spike all cut, brushed and Brillcreemed. Rusty sat real stony-eyed. Next week Spitfire comes in with his hair highlighted, honest-to-god, to look like flames on his flanks. From then on everyone began betting on the "Two Dog Match."

One day someone heard that someone else overheard Rusty making a deal in Lengby for some bear claws. Didn't take long until that got back to Dollar. Pretty soon he was out setting traps and carving deer antler buttons. No one knew for sure what those brothers were making, but the words *dog outfit* were whispered back and forth. One night I heard my ma say Snowflake was out getting wood when she saw that Old Shawl Woman crossing the road real sneaky like, taking the path towards Dollar's. *Probably helping him sew.* The rumors flew for weeks as the suspense grew. Every Tuesday more people were showing up at the center, but after the haircut and highlighting, neither brother was showing his hand.

Not that there was too much time for gawking any more on dog school days. The routines had become pretty intense. So had the owners or trainers. Each week the dogs seemed more and more in control, happier to come together for butt sniffing and tail wagging. But at the other end of the leash the frown-lines grew. Indians practiced their commands. Not just "sit" or "come" like the teacher said, of course, but "seddown, you" and "come 'ere" and lots more colorful variations, too. "Yadog" and "animosh" were called by Pudge Lakers over and over no matter how many times the dog extension class lady pleaded with them, "Please, ladies and gentlemen, use your animal's proper name so he or she doesn't become confused."

Towards the last some of us kids used to pile straw bales below the windows so we could watch the doings. It was pitiful really. All those mutts with new haircuts, new collars, and the craziest, most colorful regalia you could imagine being led around the arena by a group of people dressed in hand-me-downs and Goodwill bargains. The teachers (there were two by this time) had clipboards and pens which they mostly used for heading off the wayward dogs or pounding themselves on the head.

Only the Bush boys and three or four other owners seemed able to walk their dogs through the routine. Folks had kind of expected Rusty and Dollar would be two of the contenders. I heard how their daddy used to have some fine coon hounds and how their Uncle Benson trained and sold hunting dogs. Lots of stuff gets passed around here like that — in the family blood.

There's so many parts of those contest days that get remembered and told, but the wildest and best part was when the skunk showed up at the competition. Most everybody from the village had turned out and the teachers were too nervous to object. Even us kids talked our way in. I was on my cousin Detroit's shoulders and had a real good view. What I saw looked like some Disney nightmare or maybe a dog-America pageant. Up and down the rows, they stood, sat, or slouched, pooches of every variety. Long-hairs, short-hairs, tailed and tail-less, they wiggled with excitement, jingling or swishing, flashing the colors of their costumes. The dogs were supposed to heel in circles and in figure eights. They were to sit, lie down, stay, come, shake hands, roll over, fetch, sit up and beg.

Well it happened in the finals, during the figure eights. Rusty, Dollar, Sid Cottonwood, Toni Mae Singer, and the little LaTreque girl were in it for the money. Those who had been eliminated joined the rest of the community folks on the sidelines. Sid had just stepped out for his turn with his dog Otis. Suddenly a gunny sack flew in through a window and a skunk fought its way out. Dogs went crazy, the skunk's tail went up, and everyone raced for the door. That would have been a pretty good trick, one a person could claim after a month or so had passed. But someone must have dumped a smudge or dropped a lit cigarette in the mad dash to escape, because somehow a fire got started. Soon a couple of the dogs' costumes were flaming while the poor creatures yelped and ran in panic.

Out of the screaming and whirling colors the brothers stepped, seeming calm and walking into the very center of that tornado-force chaos. Maybe it was their army training, an instinct, or the old bond they shared, but some power entered them and stirred in them the same response. Like twin spirits they each grabbed an animal, tucked their body around it, and rolled. When they stood, marked by the smothered flames, the people in that room went silent. Just that one moment. That's how I remember it.

Then we were all outside smelling like skunk and singed hair. The Bush brothers were offered drinks and handshakes. Everyone was already busy telling what they saw. The teachers came over and they gave all that prize money to the two men, four hundred dollars a piece.

That seems like a real nice end to the story, but funny thing is the story I'm trying to get straight keeps going from there. See something happened to the Bush boys that night that made them brothers again. Some people tell how they shook hands or exchanged glances. Some say they brushed one another off and even spoke. I didn't see any of that happen.

What happened there and now in my dreams and sometimes in the stories is this: *Rusty gets up to go and Dollar follows. They walk, each with the same stride, out to Dollar's truck and he hands over a set of keys just like it hadn't been eighteen years.*

And so when folks start telling about tomato juice baths and burying all those fancy dog costumes at the dump, when I see Martha Beth performing or Possum limping down the road, I think about brooding memory and about blood. I try to figure what transforms boys into brothers or feuding brothers into heroes. I wonder what that fire purified in those two men, what burned off and what remained.

The Hungry One

an Abenaki story

as told by

Joseph Bruchac

Long ago, five people lived together in a wigwam near the River of Many Rapids. There were two small children. The boy's name was Kinosis and his sister was called Azonis. They were cared for by their loving parents Mitongwis, the father, and Nigawes, the mother. Those parents worked hard to care for their family. The fifth person who lived with them was their father's brother. All that he ever wanted to do was sleep and eat. So they called him Lazy Uncle.

Each morning, their father would go hunting. Soon after that, their mother would go to look for food plants in the forest. Then the two children would gather firewood and play while their parents were gone. And what would Lazy Uncle do? He would sit in the wigwam, close to the fire where there was food in the cooking pot. His job was to look after the children, but in truth all he ever did during the day was to sleep and eat. Every afternoon, their mother would return and start to cook and every evening, their father would return with the game he caught.

After they had all eaten, they would sit around the fire while Mitongwis and Nigawes told the old stories. The two children listened closely, for they knew there was much to be learned from the old stories. But Lazy Uncle always went to sleep before the stories were over.

One day, as Kinosis and Azonis gathered firewood near the river, they heard a little cry for help. They looked out onto the river. There, caught in a tangle of floating branches, was a little bat. It was about to drown.

"We must help that little one," said Azonis.

"I will pull that little one into shore," said Kinosis. He took a long stick, hooked the floating branches with it and did just that.

The two children freed the little bat from the tangle of branches. They placed it in the sun. Soon it was warm and dry again. It looked at them and chirped in happiness. Then it jumped up into the air, circled them four times and flew away.

One morning, as always, Mitongwis, their father, left to go hunting.

"Watch over the children," he said to Lazy Uncle, who still lay on his bed with his deerskin blanket over his head.

"I will do so," said Lazy Uncle, without moving.

Before long, Nigawes, their mother, went out to gather food plants.

"Watch over the children," she said to Lazy Uncle, who was bent over the cooking pot, scooping food out with his hand.

"I will do so," said Lazy Uncle, as he kept eating. He did not even look up when the two children, as they always did, went out to gather firewood and play.

That day, there was not as much food left in the cooking pot as usual. Before the sun was in the middle of the sky, all of the food inside the wigwam was gone. Lazy Uncle had eaten it all.

"I am hungry," Lazy Uncle said. He looked around in the wigwam, but saw nothing good to eat. He was too lazy to go outside and seek food there. Then he noticed what looked like a bone with a little meat on it. It had fallen into the glowing coals of the fire.

"That looks good to eat," Lazy Uncle said. He reached for that bone, but as he did so he burned his finger very badly.

"Ahh-heee," he said and he stuck his burned finger into his mouth to suck it. Then a smile came over his face. "This tastes gooood," he said. "I have found something gooood to eat."

Then he ate all the flesh off his finger.

"That was gooood," he said, "but I am still hungry."

Then he stuck another finger into the fire, cooked it, and ate the flesh from it.

"Yes," he said, "I have found something gooood to eat."

One by one, he cooked and ate all of his fingers. Then he cooked his toes and ate them. He cooked his arms and ate them. He cooked his legs and ate them. He cooked all the flesh on his body and ate it all and now all that was left of Lazy Uncle was a skeleton.

But he was still hungry. He looked out of the door of the lodge and saw his niece and nephew playing at the edge of the clearing. He covered himself with his deerskin blanket. Then he called up to them.

"Children," he called, in a voice that was as hard and dry as bare bones, "come heeeere, I found something good to eeeat. Come heeeere, I neeeed yooooou!"

Kinosis and Azonis looked at each other.

"Our uncle's voice frightens me," said Azonis.

"His voice sounds hard and dry as bone," said Kinosis. "We must not go into the wigwam."

So they did not do as their uncle said.

"Children," he called, again and again, "come heeere, I neeeed yoooou." But they did not come to him. And even though he was now a hungry skeleton, Lazy Uncle was still too lazy to come out and get them.

Finally, when the sun was only the width of one hand away from sunset, Nigawes came home.

"My children," she said, "why are you not in the wigwam? It will soon be dark."

"Mother," said Azonis, "something is wrong with Lazy Uncle, he has frightened us."

Just then, Lazy Uncle's voice came from the wigwam.

"Come heeeere," he called to Nigawes, "I found something good to eeeat. Now I neeeed yoooou."

"Do you hear, Mother? His voice sounds very strange," said Kinosis.

"Do not be foolish," said Nigawes. "He is your father's brother. He sounds as if he is not well. I will go see what is wrong."

The children tried to stop her, but their mother did not listen. They watched as she went to the door of the wigwam and looked inside. She could see a shape wrapped up in a deerskin blanket.

"Are you ill?" she said. She disappeared into the wigwam.

There was the sound of a loud thud and a body falling to the ground. The fire inside the wigwam grew brighter and all was quiet for a long while. Kinosis and Azonis held their breath. Then they heard the voice of Lazy Uncle once again.

"Children," Lazy Uncle said, "I found something good to eeeat again. But now I neeed yooou. Come heeere."

But Kinosis and Azonis stayed where they were. They sat with their arms around each other at the edge of the clearing as night began to fall.

Just before it was completely dark, their father came home.

"My children," Mitongwis said, "Why are you out here? It is growing cold. Let us go into our wigwam by the warm fire."

"Father," said Azonis, "we are afraid of our uncle."

"His voice is hard and cold," said Kinosis. "He told us to come inside, but we would not do so. Then our mother went into our wigwam and she has not come out again."

"Children," said Mitongwis, "do not be foolish. Lazy Uncle is my brother. Why would he want to harm us? Wait here. I will see what is wrong and then you can come inside."

The children begged their father not to go into the wigwam, but he did not listen to them. He walked to the door of the wigwam and looked in. The fire had burned down very low and it was hard to see.

"My brother," Mitongwis called, "where are you?"

"I am heeere," said the cold voice of Lazy Uncle. "Come inside. I neeed yooou."

Then Mitongwis bent his head and disappeared into the wigwam. Once more, as the children held each other tight, they heard a loud thud and the sound of a body falling. Then, as the fire burned brighter, all was quiet for a long time. Finally, they heard the hard dry voice of Lazy Uncle.

"Children," Lazy Uncle called, "I found something good to eeeat. But I am hungry again and I neeeed you. Do not come heeeere. I am coming out to get yooooou."

Frozen with terror, the children watched the door of the wigwam. They heard a sound like the sound of dry bones scraping together.

Tsschick-a-tsschick

Tsschick-a-tsschick

Tsschick-a-tsschick

Tsschick-a-tsschick

Then a tall pale shape came slowly out of the door. The moonlight glistened off its skull and its bare bones. As the hungry skeleton that had been their uncle straightened up, the two children could see its eyes gleaming like green flames. Its teeth were covered with blood.

"Children," the hungry skeleton said, "I am coming to get yooou."

Tsschick-a-tsschick

Tsschick-a-tsschick

Tsschick-a-tsschick

Tsschick-a-tsschick

He began to walk toward them. The two children jumped up and began to run, with the hungry skeleton right behind them.

Tsschick-a-tsschick

Tsschick-a-tsschick

Tsschick-a-tsschick

Tsschick-a-tsschick

They followed the trail that led next to the River of Many Rapids. As they ran, they heard a terrible scream from behind them.

"AHHH-YAAAGGGHHH"

It was the hunting cry of the hungry skeleton. The children ran as hard as they could, but it seemed as if it would soon catch them. Just then, a little shape came flying down to flutter in front of them. It was the little bat they had rescued from the river.

"Children," squeaked the little bat, "you saved me and now I must save you. Follow me."

Then the little bat led them to the place where a huge tree had fallen across the river.

"Cross here," squeaked the little bat. "Wait on the other side."

The children ran across the log to the other side. When they turned to look back, they saw the hungry skeleton standing on the river bank.

"Children, come back to meee," said the hungry skeleton. "I neeeed you."

"No," Azonis said. "We will not come to you."

"Come over here to us," said Kinosis.

"I will dooooo soooo," said the hungry skeleton.

Then it placed one bony foot onto the log and it began to walk across.

Tsschick-a-tsschick

Tsschick-a-tsschick

Tsschick-a-tsschick

Tsschick-a-tsschick

Soon it was in the middle of the log.

"Quick! Push the log into the river," squeaked the little bat.

The two children did as the little bat said. With a terrible scream, the hungry skeleton fell into the swift water and was washed away.

"Follow me," the little bat squeaked. "It is not dead yet. It will chase you again."

The little bat flew on and the two children followed. It led them along a narrow trail that wound up to the top of the high cliffs over the river. There was a deep gorge with many sharp rocks far below. At last they came to the deepest part of the gorge. There, next to the cliff, was a little wigwam. In front of that wigwam sat a short little man smoking a pipe.

"Grandfather," the little bat squeaked, "a hungry one is chasing these children. Help them."

"Are these children good children?" said the little man.

"They saved my life," said the little bat. "I have watched them sitting by the fire and listening closely to the old stories. They are good children."

"Then I must help them," said the little man.

He put down his pipe and walked to the edge of the gorge where two trees grew close together. He wrapped one leg around one tree and one leg around the other tree. Then he leaned and leaned and leaned and leaned. Each time he leaned, his body stretched until he had reached the other side. On the other side two trees grew close together. He wrapped one arm around one tree and the other arm around the other.

"Use my back as a bridge," the little man said.

Just then, a terrible cry came from nearby.

"AHHH-YAAAGGGHHH!"

"Quickly," said the little man, "the hungry one is coming up the trail. He is very close."

Kinosis and Azonis did as the little man said. They stepped onto his back to cross over to the other side. They could hear the roar of the swift water far below and they could see the moonlight on the jagged rocks. But they did not hesitate. Holding each other's hand, they crossed to the other side. As soon as the two children stepped off his back, the little man let go of one tree and let go of the other tree. Whoooooosh, he shrank back to his normal size.

The little man had just picked up his pipe again when the hungry skeleton reached the edge of the cliff.

"Little man," said the hungry skeleton, "I sssaaaw what you diiiid. Those children are miiiine. Make it sooo that I can get them."

Then the little man put down his pipe. He wrapped one leg around one tree and one leg around the other tree. Then he leaned and leaned and leaned and leaned. Just as before, each time he leaned, his body stretched until he had reached the two trees on the other side. He grabbed one tree with one hand and the other tree with the other hand.

"Now try to use my back as a bridge," he said.

"Children," said the hungry skeleton, "I am coming to get yooouuu!"

Then the hungry skeleton stepped onto the little man's back and began to walk across the gorge.

Tsschick-a-tsschick

Tsschick-a-tsschick

Tsschick-a-tsschick

Tsschick-a-tsschick

But as soon as he was in the middle, the little man let go with his hands. The hungry skeleton fell into the deep gorge with a terrible scream.

"AHHHH-YAAAGGGHHH"

It struck the sharp rocks below and shattered into many pieces.

"Children, you are safe now," the little man called over to Kinosis and Azonis. "Take that path. It will lead you home."

"But we no longer have any parents," said Azonis.

"The hungry skeleton ate them," said Kinosis.

"Children," said the little man, "is there a tall tree leaning over your wigwam?"

"Yes," said Azonis.

"That is so," said Kinosis.

"Do you remember the old stories?" said the little man. "If you do, then you will know what to do."

The two children ran home as fast as they could. By the time they got to their wigwam, the sun had risen. They looked inside. All that was left of their parents were bones. But they remembered the old stories. They ran to the base of the tall tree that leaned over the lodge and began to push. As they pushed, the tree began to fall. Then they shouted the words they had heard from the old stories.

"Mother, Father, get up quickly! A tree is about to fall on your wigwam!"

Just before the tree struck the wigwam and crushed it, their mother and father jumped out of the door. The flesh was back on their bones and they were alive and well again.

Kinosis and Azonis ran to embrace their parents.

"You have saved us," said Mitongwis.

"You have brought us back to life," said Nigawes.

So the four of them lived there near the River of Many Rapids for a long time. Their lives were very happy.

But what about Lazy Uncle, who became a hungry skeleton? That gorge where he fell onto the rocks is still there. His bones are still there among the stones. It is said that every time someone is really greedy, every time someone is really lazy, those bones come closer together.

Some nights, they say, when you walk by that gorge, you may hear a faint sound from far below. Perhaps it is the sound of Lazy Uncle, the hungry skeleton, seeking a way to get out of that gorge.

Tsschick-a-tsschick

Tsschick-a-tsschick

Tsschick-a-tsschick

Tsschick-a-tsschick

Author's Note: *The story of the greedy man or woman who becomes a hungry skeleton is widely told among the Native nations of North America. So, too, is the method of bringing bones back to life by pushing over a tall tree and shouting at them to get out of the way. This particular version of the story is based on the way the tale is told among the Western Abenaki and the Kahnawake Mohawks of northern Vermont and southern Canada. The names of the characters in the story are Abenaki names.*

Grandpa Kashpaw's Ghost

from *Love Medicine*

Louise Erdrich

You hear a person's life will flash before their eyes when they're in danger. It was him in danger, not me, but it was his life come over me. I saw him dying, and it was like someone pulled the shade down in a room. His eyes clouded over and squeezed shut, but just before that I looked in. He was still fishing in the middle of Lake Turcot. Big thoughts was on his line and he had half a case of beer in the boat. He waved at me, grinned, and then the bobber went under.

Grandma had gone out of the room crying for help. I bunched my force up in my hands and I held him. I was so wound up I couldn't even breathe. All the moments he had spent with me, all the times he had hoisted me on his shoulders or pointed into the leaves was concentrated in that moment. Time was flashing back and forth like a pinball machine. Lights blinked and balls hopped and rubber bands chirped, until suddenly I realized the last ball had gone down the drain and there was nothing. I felt his force leaving him, flowing out of Grandpa never to return. I felt his mind weakening. The bobber going under in the lake. And I felt the touch retreat back into the darkness inside my body, from where it came.

One time, long ago, both of us were fishing together. We caught a big old snapper what started towing us around like it was a motor. "This here fishing is pretty damn good," Grandpa said. "Let's keep this turtle on and see where he takes us." So we rode along behind that turtle, watching as from time to time it surfaced. The thing was just about the size of a washtub. It took us all around the lake twice, and as it was traveling, Grandpa said something as a joke. "Lipsha," he said, "we are glad your mother didn't want you because we was always looking for a boy like you who would tow us around the lake."

"I ain't no snapper. Snappers is so stupid they stay alive when their head's chopped off," I said.

"That ain't stupidity," said Grandpa. "Their brain's just in their heart, like yours is."

When I looked up, I knew the fuse had blown between my heart and my mind and that a terrible understanding was to be given.

Grandma got back into the room and I saw her stumble. And then she went down too. It was like a house you can't hardly believe has stood so long, through years of record weather, suddenly goes down in the worst yet. It makes sense, is what I'm saying, but you still can't hardly believe it. You think a person you know has got through death and illness and being broke and living on commodity rice will get through anything. Then they fold and you see how fragile were the stones that underpinned them. You see the stop signs and the yellow dividing markers of roads you traveled and all the instructions you had played according to vanish. You see how all the everyday things you counted on was just a dream you had been having by which you run your whole life. She had been over me, like a sheer overhang of rock dividing Lipsha Morrissey from outer space. And now she went underneath. It was as though the banks gave way on the shores of Lake Turcot, and where Grandpa's passing was just the bobber swallowed under his biggest thought, her fall was the house and the rock under it sliding after, sending half the lake splashing up to the clouds.

Where there was nothing.

You play them games never knowing what you see. When I fell into the dream alongside of both of them I saw that the dominions I had defended myself from anciently was but delusions of the screen. Blips of light. And I was scot-free now, whistling through space.

I don't know how I come back. I don't know from where. They was slapping my face when I arrived back at Senior Citizens and they was oxygenating her. I saw her chest move, almost unwilling. She sighed the way she would when somebody bothered her in the middle of a row of beads she was counting. I think it irritated her to no end that they brought her back. I knew from the way she looked after they took the mask off, she was not going to forgive them disturbing her restful peace. Nor was she forgiving Lipsha Morrissey. She had been stepping out on the road of death, she told the children later at the funeral. I asked was there any stop signs or dividing markers on that road, but she clamped her lips in a vise the way she always done when she was mad.

Which didn't bother me. I knew when things had cleared out she wouldn't have no choice. I was not going to speculate where the blame was put for Grandpa's death. We was in it together. She had slugged him between the shoulders. My touch had failed him, never to return.

All the blood children and the took-ins, like me, came home from Minneapolis and Chicago, where they had relocated years ago. They stayed with friends on the reservation or with Aurelia or slept on Grandma's floor. They were struck down with grief and bereavement to be sure, every one of them. At the funeral I sat down in the back of the church with Albertine. She had gotten all skinny and ragged haired from cramming all her years of study into two or three. She had decided that to be a nurse was not enough for her so she was going to be a doctor. But the way she was straining her mind didn't look too hopeful. Her eyes were bloodshot from driving and crying. She took my hand. From the back we watched all the children and the mourners as they hunched over their prayers, their hands stuffed full of Kleenex. It was someplace in that long sad service that my vision shifted. I began to see things different, more clear. The family kneeling down turned to rocks in a field. It struck me how strong and reliable grief was, and death. Until the end of time, death would be our rock.

So I had perspective on it all, for death gives you that. All the Kashpaw children had done various things to me in their lives — shared their folks with me, loaned me cash, beat me up in secret — and I decided, because of death, then and there I'd call it quits. If I ever saw King again, I'd shake his hand. Forgiving somebody else made the whole thing easier to bear.

Everybody saw Grandpa off into the next world. And then the Kashpaws had to get back to their jobs, which was numerous and impressive. I had a few beers with them and I went back to Grandma, who had sort of got lost in the shuffle of everybody being sad about Grandpa and glad to see one another.

Zelda had sat beside her the whole time and was sitting with her now. I wanted to talk to Grandma, say how sorry I was, that it wasn't her fault, but only mine. I would have, but Zelda gave me one of her looks of strict warning as if to say, "I'll take care of Grandma. Don't horn in on the women."

If only Zelda knew, I thought, the sad realities would change her. But of course I couldn't tell the dark truth.

It was evening late. Grandma's light was on underneath a crack in the door. About a week had passed since we buried Grandpa. I knocked first but there wasn't no answer, so I went right in. The door was unlocked. She was there but she didn't notice me at first. Her hands were tied up in her rosary, and her gaze was fully absorbed in the easy chair opposite her, the one that had always been Grandpa's favorite. I stood there, staring with her, at the little green nubs in the cloth and plastic armrest covers and the sad little hair-tonic stain he had made on the white doily where he had laid his head. For the life of me I couldn't figure what she was staring at. Thin space. Then she turned.

"He ain't gone yet," she said.

Remember that chill I luckily didn't get from waiting in the slough? I got it now. I felt it start from the very center of me, where fear hides, waiting to attack. It spiraled outward so that in minutes my fingers and teeth were shaking and clattering. I knew she told the truth. She had seen Grandpa. Whether or not he had been there is not the point. She had seen him, and that meant anybody else could see him, too. Not only that but, as is usually the case with these here ghosts, he had a certain uneasy reason to come back. And of course Grandma Kashpaw had scanned it out.

I sat down. We sat together on the couch watching his chair out of the corner of our eyes. She had found him sitting in his chair when she walked in the door.

"It's the love medicine, my Lipsha," she said. "It was stronger than we thought. He came back even after death to claim me to his side."

I was afraid. "We shouldn't have tampered with it," I said. She agreed. For a while we sat still. I don't know what she thought, but my head felt screwed on backward. I couldn't accurately consider the situation, so I told Grandma to go to bed, I would sleep on the couch keeping my eye on Grandpa's chair. Maybe he would come back and maybe he wouldn't. I guess I feared the one as much as the other, but I got to thinking, see, as I lay there in the darkness, that perhaps even through my terrible mistakes some good might come. If Grandpa did come back, I thought he'd return in his right mind. I could talk with him. I could tell him it was all my fault for playing with power I did not understand. Maybe he'd forgive me and rest in peace. I hoped this. I calmed myself and waited for him all night.

He fooled me though. He knew what I was waiting for, and it wasn't what he was looking to hear. Come dawn I heard a blood-splitting cry from the bedroom and I rushed in there. Grandma turnt the lights on. She was sitting on the edge of the bed and her face looked harsh, pinched-up, gray.

"He was here," she said. "He came and laid down next to me in bed. And he touched me."

Her heart broke down. She cried. His touch was so cold. She laid back in bed after a while, as it was morning, and I went to the couch. As I lay there, falling asleep, I suddenly felt Grandpa's presence and the barrier between us like a swollen river. I felt how I had wronged him. How awful was the place where I had sent him. Behind the wall of death he'd watched the living eat and cry and get drunk. He was lonesome, but I understood he meant no harm.

"Go back," I said to the dark, afraid and yet full of pity. "You got to be with your own kind now," I said. I felt him retreating, like a sigh, growing less. I felt his spirit as it shrunk back through the walls, the blinds, the brick courtyard of Senior Citizens. "Look up Aunt June," I whispered as he left.

I slept late the next morning, a good hard sleep allowing the sun to rise and warm the earth. It was past noon when I awoke. There is nothing, in my mind, like a long sleep to make those hard decisions that you neglect under the stress of wakefulness. Soon as I woke up that morning, I saw exactly what I'd say to Grandma. I had gotten humble in the past week, not just losing the touch but getting jolted into the understanding that would prey on me from here on out. Your life feels different on you, once you greet death and understand your heart's position. You wear your life like a garment from the mission bundle sale ever after — lightly because you realize you never paid nothing for it, cherishing because you know you won't ever come by such a bargain again. Also you have the feeling someone wore it before you and someone will after. I can't explain that, not yet, but I'm putting my mind to it.

"Grandma," I said, "I got to be honest about the love medicine."

She listened. I knew from then on she would be listening to me the way I had listened to her before. I told her about the turkey hearts and how I had them blessed. I told her what I used as love medicine was purely a fake, and then I said to her what my understanding brought me.

"Love medicine ain't what brings him back to you, Grandma. No. It's something else. He loved you over time and distance, but he went off so quick he never got the chance to tell you how he loves you, how he doesn't blame you, how he understands. It's true feeling, not no magic. No supermarket heart could have brung him back."

She looked at me. She was seeing the years and day I had no way of knowing, and she didn't believe me. I could tell this. Yet a look came on her face. It was like the look of mothers drinking sweetness from their children's eyes. It was tenderness.

"Lipsha," she said, "you was always my favorite."

She took the beads off the bedpost, where she kept them to say at night, and she told me to put out my hand. When I did this, she shut the beads inside of my fist and held them there a long minute, tight, so my hand hurt. I almost cried when she did this. I don't really know why. Tears shot up behind my eyelids, and yet it was nothing. I didn't understand, except her hand was so strong, squeezing mine.

The earth was full of life and there were dandelions growing out the windows, thick as thieves, already seeded, fat as big yellow plungers. She let my hand go. I got up. "I'll go out and dig a few dandelions," I told her.

Outside, the sun was hot and heavy as a hand on my back. I felt it flow down my arms, out my fingers, arrowing through the ends of the fork into the earth. With every root I prized up there was return, as if I was kin to its secret lesson. The touch got stronger as I worked through the grassy afternoon. Uncurling from me like a seed out of the blackness where I was lost, the touch spread. The spiked leaves full of bitter mother's milk. A buried root. A nuisance people dig up and throw in the sun to wither. A globe of frail seeds that's indestructible.

Dora-Rouge's bones

from *Solar Storms*

Linda Hogan

Dora-Rouge's bones were all sharp angles and she slept deeply and for long hours. I looked after her. I made it my work. At times I took her food while she was still in bed or as she sat outside in the morning sunlight. I carried her from table to bed, presented her to the sun. I felt protective of her fragile bones and thin skin. She seemed vulnerable. She became, in a way, my ward. But in spite of all this seeming frailty, the truth was that Dora-Rouge had fought gravity and won. It no longer held her as it held the rest of us. That was why she weighed so little and why she heard what no human heard and saw what none of us could see.

"Why is it you hardly ever sleep?" she asked me one day.

"I don't know." I couldn't tell her I was afraid to be held by night.

"Hand me the box under the bed."

I bent and pulled up the cover and saw the box.

"That's the one. Open it."

I did. It was full of small paper bags. In them were roots and dried leaves.

"How long has that been going on? Insomnia."

"As long as I can remember." I shrugged. I placed the box beside her. She reached inside and took out three bags. "Here, give this to Agnes. She'll cook them. It'll make you sleep."

The concoction was a mixture of roots, bark, and flowers. I was curious about the plants. There were unguents — ointments and balms — at their house, but it was the plants I wanted to know about.

"When you were a baby," Agnes told me, "all you wanted to do was look at plants. You watched the trees move when the wind blew. You listened to them and they leaned forward to tell you things."

I liked hearing this. It was the first time anyone had told me something about myself when I was a child.

One day while Dora-Rouge sat outside in the sun, and Agnes was gone to the lake, I opened one of the boxes in Dora-Rouge's room to see what it contained. It was a birch-bark box that had designs bitten into it by an ancestor's teeth. In it were some little bags, a few dried plants, and a piece of amber sitting in a bird's nest. In the amber was a frog, perfectly formed, stopped in time, its life caught in the tears of a tree. I quickly put the box back the way I'd found it. I was not going to steal out of this house. That's what they called it when I was forced to leave the yellow house for taking things. The social worker said, "Isn't this the same as running away? Isn't this another escape?"

No, I would try not to steal away from this house, dark and dreary as it was.

At night, when I rested, I would smell the fresh air, feel cool breezes on my skin, and listen to the loons and the sound of water. All these things comforted me. And with Dora-Rouge's bitter sleeping potion, I slept. Mornings, I lay awake, thinking of the words of the women, Agnes and Dora-Rouge, and wondered what I was doing there in a life so different from what I'd known. At times I felt the old fear return, the need to shed skin, to leave everything behind and run, to keep these women out of my skin. But already they were my skin, so I willed myself to remain. I tried to figure out how I could earn some money. I didn't want to live off the old people. I'd asked at Tinselman's store for work and he said there was none. I asked at the Auto Shop, Boat Repair. They, too, needed no help. There were few options.

Each evening after supper, Agnes walked to the place where the Perdition River flowed into Lake Grand. She went alone, to think, she said, and to be silent. Always she returned, refreshed and clear-eyed, as if the place where two waters met was a juncture where fatigue yielded to comfort, where a woman renewed herself.

One night, from the porch, I watched her coming back through the first shade of night. She didn't see me as she came up the road. She was half a world away in the first evening dimness. She wore the fur coat wide open and she walked with something like a dance step, even in her heavy black shoes, turning a little this way and a little that. I still remember how strong and wide her thighs appeared that night, her awkward movement. She was singing too. On her upturned face, she wore a look — half-rapture, half-pain. She was singing. I felt the song and I wanted to stay there and listen, but it was a private act, I knew. I didn't want to intrude upon Agnes' inner world, so I slipped indoors quietly, before she saw me, put water in the kettle and waited for it to heat. But all the time I smiled at her passion, her rocking movement, her bent knees.

She was still singing when she came in.

"Oh, hi," I said. Sounding stupid. And guilty. I faced the stove, waiting for the water to heat.

But Dora-Rouge, from the next room, called out, "Say, where did you hear that song?"

"I heard it inside this coat."

"I've heard it before," said Dora-Rouge. "I remember it. It's the one that calls lost things out of hiding and brings them back. But it's from before your time."

"It's the coat, Mother. I've told you that." Still humming, Agnes put a tea bag in one of the cracked cups.

"It must have been the song that called Angel back to us."

I believed Agnes about the coat. I came to think of it as something alive. When no one looked I would touch the fur and put my ear against it and listen. It was old, with no shining left to it, and silent. At least with me, when I listened.

There were mornings I sat with Dora-Rouge in her little room with the antlers and turtle-shell rattles and the box I'd snooped in. We would breathe together the way wolves do with their kith and kin, the way they nurture relations by breathing. This breath was alive. It joined us as we were joined in so many other ways. One morning as I did this, Dora-Rouge looked directly into my eyes and said, "Agnes killed that bear, you know." She sat back against the pillow with a smile. Her thin hand touched her chest, fumbling at the button of her gown. "The one she wears, it was a glacier bear."

Then I brushed her hair while she talked. The brush was old, made of ancient tortoiseshell and boar bristles. I liked the feel of her hair.

The bear was the color of ice. It was the last of its kind. It still makes me sad. It wandered down to California. No one knew why it was so far from home. But it hid out and it lived.

It was the mother, they said, of twin cubs.

There were tribes of bears in those days. They were around for thousands of years, clear back to when we lived by the laws of nature. A bear could only be killed at a certain time of year and that was for meat and medicine and fur. Even then it was a rare thing when an Indian killed a bear, because bears resemble men.

There was a Frenchman. Beauregard. He went out west to find the last of the beaver. They were mostly gone here. But it was too late. Even in California they were gone. When he saw the bear he trapped it and took it captive. At first he used it to fight dogs. The men made bets on who would win. They kept it awake all year. That's against bear nature. Its poor mind was no longer sane. And its diet was bad, so it went weak, its teeth rotted out, and some of its fur fell out in patches. Then they tried to make money by letting men wrestle the poor creature. Finally, they charged people money just to come and see it. The last one. The last glacier bear. The last. They always loved the last of anything, those men, even the last people. I guess they felt safe then, when it was all gone.

Agnes was only twelve when they brought the blue bear here. She was plump and beautiful, my girl. She was round as fruit on a tree and from the first minute she saw that bear, she loved it. It was a special thing, her and that bear. Every day she went to look at it. For a penny, they'd let her see it. A minute a penny. Some days she took thirty pennies.

When Beauregard saw how good she was with it, he hired her to feed it. He was afraid of it, you know. The other men, too. Afraid of that poor broken thing. When they went in the small cage, they kicked it away and pushed at it with their rifles. But Agnes was not afraid. She was a gentle girl. The bear liked this. It knew her, in a way. Through her eyes, I think. She stole good food for it, too, and its fur grew back.

In the afternoons, young boys would go around and poke sticks through the cage and Agnes would fight with the boys and come home crying.

Looking back on it, the boys, I think they were jealous of what's wild and strong. If the bear fought back, it was hated; if it didn't, they hated it for being weak. The bear was ruined in its heart. Even with Agnes' love. It sat with its back to the boys and let them poke it and call it names. Finally, they came to it with guns full of corn and they shot that poor bear to see if it had any fight left in its thick skin. Antagonizing it that way. Agnes cried and kicked at them. She chased after them. They called her crazy. "I'll shoot you," she said. "That's how crazy I am." She took a gun one day to keep them away. It was really just for show, the gun, but I really had to get after her for taking it. I hid it after that.

One chilly day alone, she went to the bear. She lifted her shirt and showed the bear her round, full breasts. Oh, it understood already. It knew she was a woman. It knew she had compassion.

Before she left the house that day I saw her crying. I had a bad feeling. I followed her. I watched how she entered the cage. She didn't even fear for her own life. She didn't have the gun. She only had a knife, so all the poor girl could do was cut the bear's neck and let it bleed. She did it fast, before I saw what was happening, before I could stop her.

The warm blood poured into the ground. It was a chilly day. You could see the steam rise from the wounds. Its eyes were grateful. I saw that. She stroked the big animal. I saw it with my own eyes. That bear put a paw on Agnes and stroked her in return. It touched her. It comforted her. I have never seen such a thing as that. I cried, too.

When all the life had flowed out of it, Agnes took the knife and slid it under the skin. I went to her. "What are you doing?" I said, but she didn't answer me. She knew I'd been there all along, and that I was crying. It was hard work to skin and quarter the bear. She removed the liver, the heart. She knew that bear inch by inch, where every muscle joined bone. "Don't just stand there," she told me. "Help me out." She was bossy like that, even when she was sad. "Go get the wagon," she said. "Hurry. Before they get back." The men, she meant.

I followed her orders. I rushed home. As I left I heard her singing a bear song no one had sung since I was a girl. An old, old song.

I did as she said. I went and got another knife and the bouncing wagon and when I went back, I helped pull the fur away from the flesh. I still remember the bones of the foot in a pool of blood.

Four wagonloads we brought back, bumping all the way.

That night, after dark, the Frenchman and his friend came knocking at our door. They knocked loud. They wanted the meat. Those men pushed their way into the house. "Get out!" I yelled at them. But I was scared of them. I fell back against the table. We were just women there. We had no men to protect us. They wanted the fur, too. It was a rare color for a bear. It would catch them a good price. Agnes had already pinned it. "Give me that," Beauregard said. He took it from her.

Agnes stood up to him. I couldn't believe my own eyes and ears. There were times I thought she was so stubborn, that girl, but this time I was proud of her. She stood up to him. She said, "It's all right. This fur belongs to me, but you go ahead and take it. I'll wait for you to die. You won't last, but me, I have time."

Not even a year later, he died. While his woman grieved, Agnes stole into his house *through a window and she threw the coat out onto the snow. I picked it up. She'd conned me into it, her crime, you see. I was under the window waiting. Even though I was afraid of what might happen if we got caught.*

Agnes wore the nightmare. That's what I called the coat. First thing every morning Agnes brushed the fur, rocking it in the chair, her dark hair around her plump shoulders. Like it was a baby. And talking and singing things — to this day I don't know where she got it all.

By then, the land was settled. No bears were there to disturb the people. But at night in the woods, settlers heard branches snap. They heard the breathing in the forest. The bear lived there still, and it lived inside their own skin and bones. Everything they feared moved right inside them.

Agnes wanted to know, always, why some men will do what they do. She believed wearing its skin would show her these things.

Sometimes it happens that, at twilight, I see those eyes and that large paw brushing Agnes' back and I hear her sing and I get a feeling, just a feeling, Agnes is becoming something. Maybe the bear. Maybe she knows her way back to something.

Dora-Rouge, I think now, was a root and we were like a tree family, aspens or birch, connected to one another underground, the older trees feeding the young, sending off shoots, growing. I watched and listened. It was an old world in which I began to bloom. Their stories called me home, but this home was not at all what I'd expected. I don't know exactly what it was I thought I was entering, but never would I have imagined a bear of a woman in an old, heavy coat, with bear-scratched trees outside her house, a woman who bent her creaking knees in a dance when she thought no one was looking, and boiled a kettle of the same stew nearly every night for a week, except Fridays, when she fixed macaroni and cheese in case a Catholic might stop by. Nor could I have dreamed Dora-Rouge with her handhold on the spirit world, saying grace each night by saying "Give us our daily stew." Or the mixed-blood Cree named Frenchie who lived next door and had mincing steps when she entered the house at dinnertime, uninvited but always welcome, and sat down to dinner with us.

Each Thursday, several of the town's men played cards. The Thursday before they sent me to Bush and Fur Island, the men came to Agnes' house.

Everyone knew Frenchie would show up. As she herself put it, she "had a thing" for Justin LeBlanc, an older fisherman and a regular at cards.

On that Thursday evening, Agnes looked at the clock and said, "Frenchie's late." But as Agnes pounded some tough meat into tenderness, the door opened and Frenchie sailed into the stuffy, hot kitchen, wearing a pink chiffon scarf and carrying a platter of Russian tea cookies. "What's all the racket?" she said. "You building something?"

"Supper," was all Agnes said.

Frenchie was dressed for dinner, wearing a red dress and too much color on her cheeks. She smelled of face powder and wore a strand of pearls around her withered neck. Without bothering to untie her tennis shoes, she pushed them off her feet, then walked barefoot to the stove and peered inside the kettle. "Stew," she said, as if we didn't know.

Agnes' efforts to soften the meat had been in vain — the gristly meat was a failure and later, as Dora-Rouge sipped broth and marrow, she watched us trying to chew and said, "You make me grateful I don't have any teeth."

And just before the dishes were stacked and washed, Justin pulled up. Seeing his car, Frenchie ran to the bathroom to check her hair and spray lilac cologne on her neck.

The men all smoked pipes that year and before long the pipe smoke filled the house in a comforting sort of way. I was still uneasy there but I liked the men's voices as they talked and drank glasses of cola and ate peanuts. And I liked the smoke better than the perfume. I'd never heard men talk that way before, like friends. All the places I'd been, men didn't have friends.

For the first time — I met LaRue. LaRue Marks Time was his name, although some people called him "Done Time" behind his back. At other times, people shunned him, but he was a good hand at cards. He wore a gray shirt and his hair long, in a thin ponytail down his back. He was handsome, his hair beginning to gray at the temples, but for some reason I was uncomfortable in his presence. He, on the other hand, was eager to befriend me. "How about I take you fishing tomorrow," he volunteered.

"Okay. Sure," I sounded nervous. He didn't seem quite sincere. I didn't know then that he wanted to befriend me so he could get close to Bush. I didn't yet know I would soon live with Bush, the woman of Fur Island.

"Here, I have something for you." He reached into his pocket and brought out an arrowhead, warm with his body heat.

I studied his face. I looked at the arrowhead, then slipped it into my pocket.

"When are you going to the island?" he asked.

"What island?" This was the first I heard.

"You know, to Bush's." He straightened his collar, hitched up his jeans.

I was hurt, thinking that Agnes and Dora-Rouge were sending me away.

"I'll tell you about it later," Agnes said, seeing my discomfort.

Later that night the women retreated into the living room, but we could hear the sound of pennies sliding across the table, the shuffling of cards, and the warm sound of men's voices. Now and then Frenchie would walk through the door and offer cookies to the men, who never accepted. I could see her through the doorway. She smiled too much at Justin. He would pretend to be cranky and disturbed by her. "Are you telling them my hand?" he accused her.

"You know me better than that," she said with a gleam in her eye.

I listened, but still I thought of what LaRue had said, that I would leave the Rib. For the first time in my life I didn't want to go.

The men spoke in different ways from the women. Their conversations went something like this: "Have you ever caught a bluefish? Those are something else. They go out, oh, about a hundred yards and you have to bring them back. They've got a lot of teeth. They look like tuna or something."

"Yeah, they give you a good battle."

Fish stories. And they talked loud.

"I fished until four in the morning," one would say. "And I couldn't catch a thing."

Now, I know this probably meant he'd caught so many he wanted to keep the place a secret. That's how they talked, in a circular fashion.

"Next time let's take some bacon. I heard they really strike at that."

"Yeah. Or salmon eggs. They like them, too."

"Where is Devil's Lake, anyway?"

"My uncle went there. He did real good."

"Red hots. I hear they bite at those, too."

"Is that the uncle that got struck by lightning three times?"

In the living room, which doubled as my bedroom, the teapot sat on the old gold-painted sewing machine and the women talked with one another. They talked about the deepest things, the most meaningful of subjects, about love and tragedy. Frenchie said she'd once loved a younger man. Agnes said she still thought of her son Harold and what had come of him. Dora-Rouge, propped up next to me on the cot, said, "I want to go home to die. It's my dream. It is so beautiful there. When I was young, the northern lights would dance, really dance across the sky. They were so close to us. When we saw them we'd say, 'Here comes sky on its many trails.'

"When I met Luther, he was just a boy. He came to sit with us. That's how it was done in those days. He'd just sit. A girl would ignore a boy who was coming to court her. She had to hide her smile. So would her family. And Luther'd come and sit. Then one day, I looked at him and smiled. After that, he started bringing meat to the house."

I cut a piece of cheese and handed it to her. She kept it in her mouth until it was soft enough to swallow. "Is that Wisconsin cheese?" she said. And that's how the talk went with the women. That is, until Frenchie pushed the plate of cookies toward me and said, "What happened to your face, anyway, dear?" She said it straight out. The forbidden question when I was younger. I had left schools for people's curiosity. I'd moved out of the houses, run away as if I were running from ugliness or pain. It was what no one was allowed to say. Even I had stopped asking about it. At first I'd tried to find out what had caused the scars, but eventually I gave up. Now I was stopped dead cold, but it seemed I was the only one who heard Frenchie. Not even a moment of silence elapsed — the women kept chatting — but my heart raced with fear. I felt the color drain from my face. I sat stunned.

"Well?" Frenchie looked at me briefly, ignorant of her transgression, then said, "Maybe I should take some cookies to Justin." She rose from the chair to peer anxiously into the next room. Justin's back was toward her.

To hide my feelings, I tried to cut another piece of cheese for Dora-Rouge, but my hands shook and it slipped and I cut my finger, a deep bit off the tip.

Agnes stood up. "Come, let's fix that up." She was anxious. I think she noticed how my heart had fallen.

I pulled away from her. "It's okay," I said. I wrapped a napkin around it. "Really. It's fine." My eyes were beginning to tear.

"No, that's a worthless, rusty knife. Let's clean that wound."

I said, "No," but Agnes guided me into the washroom. Finally I let her. I nearly collapsed against her, as if the cut had been deeper, but it was the words that had hurt me, not the knife.

Agnes knew this.

She opened the medicine cabinet and took out gauze and adhesive tape and when I smelled that odor, something inside me began to move around, the memory of wounds, the days and weeks of hospitals, the bandages across my face, the surgeries. Or maybe it was the look of blood in the sink that hit me, the red, iron-filled water that had stained everything, even the insides of myself in the mirror, and suddenly, without warning, I hit the mirror with my hand, hit the face of myself, horrified even as I did it by my own action, that I would go so far as to break the mirror, the cabinet containing iodine, Mercurochrome, Merthiolate, Wild Root Oil. Glass shattered down into the sink and broken pieces spread across the floor, settling in corners. I heard a voice yelling "Damn it!" and it was me, my own voice, raging and hurt. There was anger in it, a deep pain, and the smell of hospitals of the past, the grafts that left my thigh gouged, the skin stolen from there to put my face back together. That was part of it, of what lay broken and sharp in the sink and on the floor. And I felt sick. I leaned over the toilet.

"What's going on?" yelled Dora-Rouge. And Frenchie was right outside the closed door. "Are you girls okay in there?"

Agnes called me honey and sweetheart and child. "Shhhh. It's okay." She held me. I sobbed helplessly. Me, the girl who never cried. When I stood up and looked, I saw that the sink was filled with cut, broken reflections of my face. I tried to clean up the glass, to pull myself together. "We'll get it later," Agnes said. "Let's go out and get some air."

"I'm sorry," I said. "I'm so sorry." I held on to her, my wet face in her shoulder. I didn't want to leave that little bathroom with its iron-stained sink and pieces of glass. I didn't want to face the others.

Then I said, "You don't want me. You're sending me to an island."

"It's all right," she said. "You'll be able to come back any time you want."

"You didn't even tell me."

Agnes' voice was comforting, but it took all my courage to be willing to leave the room. I was still shaken and sobbing when Agnes opened the bathroom door and all the men stood outside it with their arms hanging lifeless at their sides, Husk in his white shirt and black suspenders. All of them looked at me, LaRue with his mouth open. Finally the silence was broken when Husk smiled and said, "Way to go!" He chewed on some peanuts, nodded at me, and laughed, then picked up a bottle of Coke from the table and toasted me. "Thatta girl, Angel. Those things are the source of vanity."

His words saved me from embarrassment. They were generous, quick-thinking words. The men smiled and turned and sat down to cards again, as if nothing had happened. "I'll raise you thirty cents," Justin said, hunched over like an old dark bird, squinting from the year when he'd been snow-blinded, 1942, when he was out on a trapline and injured his ankle.

Agnes and I stepped out of the bathroom and walked into the first of autumn darkness, together.

We sat side by side on a rock near the place where the river entered the lake, and I who had not cried as a child, not even at the taunting of other children, wept.

"She's like that, Frenchie is. It's her way. You get used to it."

Down on the lake, the light of a fisherman opened through darkness like an eye that peered at me and caught me without my face of toughness. I turned away, so nothing or no one could see me. Agnes put the bear coat over my shoulders, her arm about me, folding me in. "When I wear this coat, Angel, I see the old forests, the northern lights, the nights that belong to something large that don't know."

That night after the card game, after the silent walk back up the road with Agnes, I was both relieved and heavy with weariness; I felt freed of something I couldn't name. Later, I undressed in the dark, close room of the house that breathed with the sleep of others and when I slept I dreamed I fell over the edge of land, fell out of order and knowing into a world dark and primal, seething, and alive as creation, like the beginning of life.

I began to form a kind of knowing at Adam's Rib. I began to feel that if we had no separate words for inside and out and there were no boundaries between them, no walls, no skin, you would see me. What would meet your eyes would not be the mask of what had happened to me, not the evidence of violence, not even how I closed the doors to the rooms of anger and fear. Some days you would see fire; other days, water. Or earth. You would see how I am like the night sky with its stars that fall through time and space and arrive here as wolves and fish and people, all of us fed by them. You would see the dust of sun, the turning of creation taking place. But the night I broke my face there were still boundaries and I didn't yet know I was beautiful as the wolf, or that I was a new order of atoms. Even with my own eyes I could not see deeper than my skin or pain in the way you cannot see yourself with closed eyes no matter how powerful the mirror.

My ugliness, as I called it, had ruled my life. My need for love had been so great I would offer myself to any boy or man who would take me. This was, according to women who judged me, my major sin. There was really no love in it, but I believed any kind of touch was a kind of love. Any human hand. Any chest to lean my head against. It would heal me, I thought. It would mend my heart. It would show my face back to me, unscarred. Or that love would be blind and ignore my face. But the truth remained that I was wounded and cut and no one could, or would, tell me how it happened and no man or boy offered what I needed. And deep down I dreaded knowing what had happened to me and the dread was equal to my urgent desire to learn the truth. Once, asking a foster mother what had happened to my face, there was silence. She and her husband looked at each other. "You fell," she said, and I knew she lied.

But I was like Agnes had said: Water going back to itself. I was water falling into a lake and these women were that lake, Agnes, with her bear coat, traveling backward in time, walking along the shore, remembering stories and fragments of songs she had heard when she was younger and hearing also the old songs no one else remembered. And Dora-Rouge, on her way to the other world, already seeing what we could not see, answering those we could not hear, and, without legs, walking through clouds and waters of an afterlife.

Aboriginal

Australia

Who Took the Children Away?

Richard Frankland

The match misses the bin, I load up and flick again. Miss. The TV is blaring, some fantasy world with a guy who looks not only like he stepped out of a magazine, but also so smart he could get a couple of doctorate degrees. He's solving forty-five murders an hour, walking off with the girl and driving a Porsche on a cop's wage. I stand and look around the motel room. I look at the phone, no one to ring. Look at the paper, the work I do is all over the front page again. Don't want to read it, they always miss the point anyway. I stare at Mr Beautiful on TV and laugh.

I grab hold of my briefcase and decide to look through the investigation papers; statements collected about lives, they tell a different story from the official one. All of a sudden I can hear an aunty's voice. "He was a great horseman and drover. Well known in Moama and Echuca, everyone liked him. Men like him were really great men. Way they've been coming across in the Royal Commission hearings, you'd think they were just nobodies. As if nobody wants them, that they were unloved. That's not true, they were dignified men — he was a gentleman."

I close my eyes and see a young black man riding as if born to the saddle, wheeling his horse with great skill, guiding cattle. He flashes me a grin as he cuts yet another one out and skilfully brings his horse to a halt. I think he's gunna talk to me — but the hero on TV brings me back to the motel room. He's solved another murder, killed everyone and got another girl.

I flick idly through the statements, shaking the sleep from my head, and light another cigarette. The guy on the TV is smiling at me through the credits. Not a hair out of place even though he's just saved the world. I give him the finger, say he wouldn't know if his arse was on fire, but he keeps on smiling.

I lie back and think of a train ride that led to death and the questions of a grieving family. "He'd committed no crime, other than yelling out that he'd missed his station. Can't understand why he was placed in a prison cell." He'd served his country. At one time that old man was a soldier. I easily fall through time and see a young man in uniform. He's playing two-up behind a shed. There's a group with him, mostly white, but they don't seem to see his colour. He's got them all laughing at something. I walk closer as he throws the coins in the air. He looks at me, smiling, and points to the coins. I look up and the coins become lost in the glare of the fluoro light of my motel room.

No more, I think, don't think no more, it'll send you crazy. I sit up and look at the videos I picked up from reception. I grab one at random and throw it in the machine. I stand to draw the curtains, my thoughts absorbed by the darkness outside, when the phone rings, startling me. I stare at it with contempt before answering it. It's reception reminding me to put in my breakfast order. I silently question their motives. Have they done it out of kindness or for my money? I'm paranoid, I keep telling myself, they don't all hate us. "Very co-operative and well mannered for a Black Deaths in Custody interviewing officer." No, I think, they don't all hate us, they just can't see their own racism.

The world of video has me in its thrall and I watch the previews leading into the movie. A slowly building theme song has started and the music pushes me back so that I'm knocking on the front door of a house. It's a beautiful day and rock music is playing loudly somewhere inside. I can hear kids laughing the way that only kids can, and a flustered young mum answers my knocking.

The music has stopped now and we are sitting inside looking at photographs of a young man, he has clear eyes and a strong look. He's standing in front of a truck proudly showing it to the world. She's explaining to me what that truck meant to them and a single tear begins to form as their dreams lie shattered in her memory. One of the kids bursts into the room and I see how much he looks like his dad.

On the TV, the hero and his sidekick have burst into a room to capture any crooks or villains that may be hiding. I wonder about those heroes — what would they do in my situation? Could they even identify the villains, villains who don't wear masks, not the kind you see on TV anyway.

I light another cigarette and my eye catches the breakfast order. I fill it out then put on a jacket — it's cold out — and walk to reception. There's a pub in the distance, maybe a hundred yards, it looks like it's open. I decide to go for a drink. I'm shaking now and I can't work out whether it's the cold or my nerves.

I walk down the road towards the pub and stop to light a smoke. The pub carpark has about half a dozen cars in it. A slamming car door and muffled voices break the silence of the night. I think of sitting in my car listening to someone whose brother has died tell me "thanks, thanks". I think, for what? I haven't solved anything, haven't resolved anything, not even close. I accept the thanks anyway and he shakes my hand, places a leather headband in it. I look behind him and see a prison officer and a minimum security prison sign. He can't come with me, he's in jail. Later I tie the headband to my guitar, and it stays there for years.

I walk through the pub door. Like all country pubs everyone looks as you come in. A little hostility in their eyes and manner — don't ask me how, but I can feel it. I ignore them and walk straight to the bar and order a scotch and Coke, short glass, no ice, but not too much Coke. The barman silently takes my order and my money. Everyone else resumes their conversations and I concentrate on my drink, trying to escape the ghosts.

"You an Aborigine, are ya?"

The voice comes from a weather-beaten face. Silently I nod my head, I have heard this a thousand times before.

"I grew up with your people." He looks at me smilingly for approval.

I take a sip and smile back, with the rest of the pub looking on. Having proved his credentials, he's now going to take the opportunity to claim a degree in Aboriginality — probably regards himself as the local authority. What power I wield. He looks over his shoulder to check that everyone has seen my nod. Satisfied, he turns back to me.

"They were all right back then."

I wearily stare at him.

"Bloody good footy players..."

Silent reflection as he delves into his memory for more accolades about my race. I think about how he'd react if I told him that footy is a Koori game...and what he'd do if I said I had just come from taking statements from some of my people about how some of his people had imprisoned them. That many of them had died.

"Good on the knuckle too..." Some of the pub have lost interest and he glances over his shoulder in panic, realising he must do something to regain their attention. "Drink too bloody much though."

I look at him, taking in his bulbous nose and broken veins. His peers, now sitting in silent disarray, look at me, waiting for my reaction. I knock back my scotch and order another. I want to grab these guys by the back of the head and run them through my life, run them through the stories coming out of the Royal Commission, just so they can see the horror and despair, the hate, the anger, the dispossession. I want them to wear my shoes, to live my life just once, just so they know.

I want to turn their heads around so they look at themselves, sitting there pissed while their wives are at home with the kids, while the front page blares out how hard the farmers are doing it. One of his mates yells out — saving me from having to answer, saving me from having to justify my existence yet again. Relieved, I light another cigarette and let the scotch take effect.

I decide to have one more. The barman answers my summons and tentatively smiles, the smile disappearing as fast as my money. I think of another smile, a gentle smile from a young girl talking about her uncle. How he could protect her and her family, how he was taken away at the age of eleven, how he came home after not seeing his family for some incredible amount of years, and how he loved them.

I think of how he died — lost in a religion that never really forgave him — lying on a toilet floor with a paintbrush protruding from his eye. And I think of her tears, the way she quietly sobbed her hurt to me and how helpless I felt.

I drink my scotch, faster this time, and feel it warm me against the cold. The blokes in the pub are ignoring me now, I don't seem to be a threat to them. The mood in the room has long passed that stage where you feel claustrophobic — I'm feeling reckless anyway. But I ignore the other drinkers, there's no way they could live in my world, they could never know my world — but I know theirs.

I finish my drink and walk outside, the fresh air sending cold fingers into my lungs. I hope that I can sleep tonight. In the distance I can see the motel and notice that the reception has closed. I realise that I haven't put in my breakfast order, it's still in my pocket. A song starts in my head, it's Archie Roach singing about taking the children away. I look back at the pub and think of the guy at the bar who thinks he knows everything about my people. I wonder if he would have taken the children away.

Night Games

Kenny Laughton

We were really excited, me and big brother.

Ung Ung was taking us bush for the weekend. We were going back to school, not whitefella way, not times table and alphabet. No, we would hunt, learn how to track and dig out atyunpe, the juicy perentie, and eat his fat; good medicine too, that fat.

And Ung Ung would get us to climb the ilwempe, them old ghost gums, home of a sought-after bushtucker, those big white grubs, tyape the witchetty. Didn't like them raw, bit yucky, but had to eat them when Ung Ung said so. Just put em in my mouth, bite em off at the head and swallow them in one gulp. Didn't like chewing em, not raw. But rolled in the coals of a dying fire, now that was a different matter. We would watch them squirm and sizzle like a sausage on a barbecue. They would straighten right out when cooked, turn grey-black. Yum, didn't mind chewing them then, bit like egg, an omelette I suppose.

Ung Ung knew when to go bush.

Good rains not long ago — bushtucker everywhere. Wouldn't have to take much food — alangkwe the wild banana and arrutnenge the passionfruit, they would be plentiful. Maybe take a bit of merne.

And tinned corned beef. Ung Ung loved his tin meat.

Even though he'd take a rifle to hunt the ferals — rabbit or goat — and our tucker the aherre and there would be plenty of kere, we'd still have some tins of bully beef all right. Just habit I guess. Ung Ung had worked his traditional lands for them pastoralists year in and year out and must have got a taste for that tinned beef. The station mob thought of him as just a ringer, even though they did admit he was one of the best trackers and horsemen they had ever seen. Even named him after the station owner. We knew better, Ung Ung was our teacher — he was custodian of our ancestors' stories — and he was taking us bush. No wonder we were excited.

Dad had already fuelled up his trusty old FJ Holden. Our swags, tuckerbox, billycans and water containers were jammed into the gaping mouth of the boot, then slammed shut in haste, in case something tried to push itself out.

Ung Ung and Dad were laughing and talking — sometimes English, sometimes Arrernte. My young ears strained to decipher both languages, but there was too much interference, too many distractions — like big brother jabbing me in the ribs and putting a headlock on me. My ears were burning and I tried to pull away. Our legs tangled and we wrestled to the ground. He was too strong for me and thought it was funny, hurting me. Ung Ung saw it on my face and leant over and clipped big brother behind the ears — not hard, but with authority nonetheless. "Come on, leave your little brother alone, we gotta go now." Big brother let me go and got up grinning — confident and cheeky. I breathed a sigh of relief as the choking clamp of his arm was finally released from around my throat.

I was still catching my breath, panting, when big brother shaped up again, ready for another round. I tried to block him as he clipped me a few times, sending sharp stinging jabs to my face. I felt the rage rise rapidly inside me. I wanted to fight him, to hurt him back, but I knew he could flog me, already had plenty of times. I swore I'd get him one day, even if I had to use a big stick, I'd get him, no worries. Luckily, Dad intervened, grabbing big brother by his shirt collar and slapping him on the backside. "Enough of that now, get in the car or you can stay home!" Must have found the magic words, cos big brother became an instant angel.

Finally we were all packed and ready to go. Dad fired up the engine of the old car, made his way past the thistle pines and cedar trees that hugged the boundaries of our yard and onto the narrow bitumen highway that led out of town. My old man steered the car towards the break in the ranges known as the Gap. Soon we were through and Dad turned sharp left off the highway and onto a dusty, even narrower dirt track. We crossed the ancient, usually waterless, Todd River and turned east, heading towards our traditional country, to another break in the ranges, a place the whitefellas called Arltunga Gap. It was a nice relaxing drive following the road as it twisted its way through acres of mulga and saltbush. There was plenty of room in the back seat for me and big brother and we had a door each to stare out of. Big brother had one arm hanging outside the door and he stuck his face into the brisk breeze that ricocheted off the travelling vehicle.

I copied him and thought I was just it.

After about ten minutes of squinting into the breeze and blinking at the billowing dust that was being whipped up by the tyres, I stuck my head back into the relative sanctuary of the back seat. Big brother looked over at me and grinned. He pointed at my face and began to laugh. I looked back, puzzled at first, wondering what mischief big brother was up to now but then he indicated to me to look in the car's rear vision mirror.

I did and saw what had made my brother giggle.

The wind had blown my hair almost fan-like and dust had settled on the sweat areas around my eyes and lips. The layers of dust made me look like a clown with a painted face and wig. I didn't care how I looked. We were going bush and I was having a ball already, I just loved being out in the scrub. The old car rolled on, steadily getting closer to its destination. I stared out of the window and soaked up the magic of the MacDonnell Ranges as they spread out for miles either way like a chain of fossilised caterpillars. As the sun began its gradual descent in the west they began to give off a reddish glow.

We arrived several hours before sunset, so had plenty of time to unload the car and set up our weekend camp. Dad parked on the bank of the dry, sandy creek that swept through Arltunga Gap like a waterless highway, its white sands providing a comfortable bed for our swags. Ung Ung found a big gum tree with plenty of branches and leaves that would shield us from the harsh rays of the sun during the day.

We gathered light mulga branches and stumps to start a fire and me and big brother, showing off, dragged over some big ironwood logs to burn later. These were the slow burners, good steady heat with great coals for damper and cooking meat, and you didn't have to keep getting up at night to stoke the fire.

Me and big brother jumped up and down and waved vigorously as Dad drove away. "Aretyenhenge, aretyenhenge — see you later," we called out. He responded by beeping the horn several times until the old car disappeared from sight, swallowed up by a swirling pool of dust that appeared as if by magic. It was as if the ancient ones had conjured it up to whisk Dad and his old car back home.

Me and big brother wanted to go hunting.

We were impatient yet we knew that if we were good, and we usually were with Ung Ung, he would give us a shot out of his single action .22 rifle. Maybe we could knock a couple of rabbits over, I hoped so anyway. But first we had to learn some more schooling — bush lessons. We climbed the steep cliff face that rose abruptly from the edge of the river. Ung Ung had looked for and found the spear tree. It was dark green and bushy, with elongated, almost half circle-like limbs reaching out from the base of the tree.

Ung Ung used a small hatchet and cut away half a dozen of the bendy branches. They were all similar in length, about six or seven feet long and about an inch thick. We gathered them up and carried them back down the cliff to our camp at the base of the big gum tree.

Ung Ung made me put the billy on so we could have a cup of tea. Big brother got the task of cleaning the rifle. He removed the magazine and bolt so that the pull-through, lightly touched with cleaning oil, could be inserted. Then he dragged it through the barrel, leaving it glistening and smooth, ready to launch the first bullet.

Our tasks completed, Ung Ung would now teach us how to make the spears. He picked up one of the bendy branches, took a throwing stance and flicked it several times, watching it quiver in response to his actions. He nodded his head approvingly several times and said, "Good weight this one, feels good." He squatted on the ground near the fire and began to peel back the bark to expose the smooth white flesh of the wood. This released the pungent aroma of the sap that seeped out from the bark and wood. The old man dropped the branch onto the creek bed and began to rub the smooth sand over the branch, rubbing vigorously to remove the smell and the dampness of the sap. Satisfied that the wood was dry enough, Ung Ung began to pass the branch slowly back and forth through the flames of the fire, stopping briefly to clamp the wood in his teeth, bite it several times then run it through the flames again, repeating the process over and over.

We did it too, copying Ung Ung almost religiously.

The wood tasted bitter to me and it had a smell of burnt ash and smoke about it, but it was working, I could see the transformation. Somehow it reminded me of them witchetty grubs cooking in the coals — that same grey-black colour, and the way they stiffened and straightened from the heat of the fire. Maybe that's how the ancient ones got the idea for straightening the spear trees. I dunno really, but I could make that connection, especially now. I looked through the gap to the saltbush-laden plain on the other side. Big mob of rabbits over there, I knew cos I'd been there before.

Suddenly the closeness of the gap grabbed me, almost shook me to wake me up.

This was my grandfather's country, his Dreaming, his story. The paintings were there etched in ochre on the granite of the cave walls. I didn't know the stories, not yet anyway, but I knew it was my grandfather's country so I felt safe, I belonged here.

Soon the spears were done and Ung Ung was satisfied. We could hunt now. Big brother carried a backpack. Inside was a small car battery that was connected to a spotlight. He would spot the rabbits and Ung Ung would shoot them. Me, I was the gatherer, the "picker-upper", and if the bunnies were wounded I had to finish them off — with a chop to the back of the head with my hand, karate style. I would have preferred to hit them with a stick cos it hurt my hand after a while, but that's how Ung Ung told me to do it. And I didn't want to tell them that it hurt my hand, anyway, especially big brother, he would tease me and call me a sook.

Don't know why I loved my big brother, but I did.

Before long Ung Ung tracked a big perentie. We could see the tell-tale marks left by his feet and tail, like signposts in the desert sands. He was full up too. Must have had a feed of baby rabbits or birds, its bloated belly grazed a trail along the ground. We found him soon enough and Ung Ung dug its hole out until we could see the familiar spotted yellow and ochre tail of the atyunpe.

But he didn't pull it out. No, not Ung Ung. He made me do it, and I wasn't really keen on doing this myself! It was a bit scary and felt strange as I grabbed hold of the tail and slowly slid my hand along the perentie's back until I got hold of its neck. The skin was rough, almost gristly, and it made my hair stand up. I held its neck so tight I reckon I almost choked it, and my other hand held it at the base of the tail and back legs. No way that atyunpe was going to bite or scratch me. And I pulled and pulled; but that big old lizard didn't want to budge from that hole. The harder I tried to pull him out, the more he dug his claws into the dirt.

In the end Ung Ung dug out around the hole until it was completely exposed. We pulled him out okay then. Ung Ung took that atyunpe from me, grabbed it around the throat and flicked it once, snapping its neck. Killed it stone dead.

We shot half a dozen rabbits, including one each by me and big brother. Ung Ung said we had enough, we could go back to camp and have a good feed. We'd been out for a couple of hours and I was hungry, and sure was looking forward to another cup of tea. Funny how tea always tastes better out bush — out of a billycan, steaming hot, straight into a pannikin, couldn't beat it.

Big brother, he carried that pack with the battery and spotlight all that time, didn't complain or want to offload it once. He was strong all right and he loved going bush as much as I did. He shone the spotlight to guide us back through the gap in the ranges. Soon we could see the glow of our camp fire. Figures danced weirdly on an unlikely screen, the trunk of that big old gum tree. It frightened me a bit — wasn't that keen on the dark. And to add to this niggling feeling in my stomach, a night hawk let out a long piercing screech that seemed to echo and bounce along the shadowy walls of the now unrecognisable mountain range.

The fire was close now, it warmed me inside and out and that niggling feeling started to fade.

Ung Ung carried two rabbits, that old atyunpe and his rifle. I had carried four rabbits and was glad to drop them onto the wide rounded root of the gum tree. Ung Ung would soon prepare them for cooking — cut little slits in the belly, pull out the guts and sew it back up with a small green stick. He'd then singe the hair on the rabbits and the skin of the atyunpe, scrape it all off then cook them in the coals. I began to swallow my spit just thinking of it. I chucked some more wood on the fire and filled the billycans up; good cup of tea wouldn't be far off.

I had been staring aimlessly into the fire, must have been miles away. I glanced up as the flames danced and whirled like some unrehearsed corroboree, whipped up and fuelled by the fresh logs and branches that I had added to make enough coals to cook our hunting haul.

It was then that I noticed the change in Ung Ung.

In the comforting glow of the fire I saw his face clearly; but I became increasingly apprehensive when Ung Ung's old eyes widened and his head turned slowly from side to side, scanning the darkness beyond the light of the fire.

Gees, it frightened me. I'd never seen that look on Ung Ung's face before. That niggling feeling that had been gnawing at me earlier returned to my sides in an instant.

Even big brother finally noticed, and he wasn't so tough then either. He grabbed hold of me and held me tight. I was too afraid to speak. I wanted to ask Ung Ung what the matter was, what had caused the deep furrows now etched on his brow but the words wouldn't come out, no matter how hard I tried.

Big brother finally worked up enough courage to speak, but even then it came out in a frightened whisper. "What's the matter Ung Ung? Something..." He didn't finish the sentence as Ung Ung cut him off. A long slow "Sssssssh" pierced the night and he signalled for silence with a finger to his lips.

I was consumed by real fear now.

All I wanted to do was grab the rifle and start shooting. Didn't matter that I didn't know what was there or couldn't see anything. Just hearing that rifle going off would be a comfort, maybe scaring something in the dark. Something that was scaring the hell out of me right then.

Ung Ung moved over to us slowly and picked up the spotlight.

He flicked it on and shone it on our swags and the tucker box. I had opened the box when we first got back and taken out the tea but hadn't really looked inside properly. Now I could see that all the tucker was gone — four loaves of bread, the flour for the damper, even Ung Ung's treasured tins of bully beef. I was really puzzled and wanted to ask Ung Ung what was up but he was concentrating hard.

He shone the light around the fire and our campsite. The footprints in the sand were clear and they were definitely ours. There were no impressions of anything else, not even a bird or lizard. How come our tucker was gone? Now Ung Ung tilted his head back slightly and sniffed the air. Instinctively, I did the same and the stench hit my nostrils immediately — a strong, almost choking smell of sweat. My sense of fear was heightened when Ung Ung said quietly, "Something no good here — we gotta go now."

That niggling feeling turned to pure panic.

I wanted to cry but clung tight to big brother — he could have given me a hiding there and then and I still wouldn't have let go. Ung Ung shone the spotlight again, in a wider arc this time, searching the nearby mulga trees, the base of the range and through the gap. He directed the light up the big tree we were standing under then finally out towards the riverbank and the dirt road that led back home. Suddenly the light flickered and faded and began to glow dimly — it was going flat! Ung Ung grabbed his rifle, slipped the magazine in and slid the bolt back and forth, engaging a bullet and pushing it into the barrel.

He signalled to us to move, and move we did. No messing around here, we left everything — couldn't get away fast enough — no words, just haste. That old man walked swiftly as he guided us onto the track that led us home; and I lengthened my stride to keep up with him and big brother. No way was I going to dawdle that night, I positioned myself strategically between Ung Ung and big brother and I didn't slacken my pace, nor did I look back even once to that mysterious blackness we had departed from. It took us most of the night to walk back home and hardly a word was spoken between the three of us. It was one of the darkest, scariest nights I can ever remember.

Even though I was so afraid to really ask what was going on, by the time we finally got home, I was so exhausted all I wanted to do was sleep. But sleep would not come easy this night. I rolled uncomfortably through short, sharp, mixed up dreams. Giant crimson coloured nighthawks, their thunderous screeches blasting off granite walls as they dived at a tremendous speed to try and catch me.

Twice I was almost taken and then...

The dream changed. I was running along that same dark twisting track we had walked tonight. But I was on my own, no Ung Ung, no big brother and I was scared. I prayed to gods known and unknown as I ran down this black, seemingly endless path.

But still they came...those ancients of the dark.

Blasting out of the surrounding blackness, their ghost gum like features, with flowing hair and grey beards, adding to their already fearsome appearance. My little legs pumped hard to put enough distance between them and me. But it was to no avail. No matter how hard I ran, they got closer and soon they began to throw their glowing hunting spears. I ran, I dodged, I weaved, I did everything I could to avoid those eerie neon lances that sparkled and crackled as they hissed past me.

I woke up with a start and I was covered in sweat and shaking uncontrollably.

But now I thought I knew the answer to much of what had troubled me this night.

No one told me but I knew I had been in the presence of a feather foot; we had crossed paths with the legendary kadaicha man. I was scared just thinking of the danger. I knew the events of this night would remain with me.

But now I really was exhausted and all I wanted to do was sleep. And sleep I did — with the light on of course!

let me tell you what I want

Melissa Lucashenko

I had thought to be immune to love, but which of us is ever that? My brother, a case in point. He was born dark-lashed and honey-skinned and all the little white nurses sighing for him before his first hour was up. He's a man now, and walks down the street as all men, black or white, must do; it's not his fault that hearts shatter as he passes. You can hear them going off in the cafes and newsagents — boom boom what was that? — as another young woman slumps to the floor. I'm not really sure what happened, she tells the ambulance man, I had a terrible pain here, under my breast, and then I doubled over, I can't explain it, it's never happened before. Her forehead is creased by the whole business. She can't explain it, but I can.

Men follow him home sometimes. They stand on the footpath, all handsome and forlorn, till I send them away. Or maybe he pulls the curtain aside and looks, and says all right. Then roses come the next day; oh, he always comes up smelling of roses, my brother.

You should be a model, they tell him, the very boldest daring to touch a cheekbone.

Why not get into politics, they tell him, their eyes all agleam.

We're looking for someone, they say. Someone for a band, for a short film, for a share house, for a trip to Darwin, for a piece of avant-garde dadaesque theatre, for a job in someone's landscape gardening business, for a short-order chef, for a drug courier, for a —

They never say what they really want. They never say they're looking for love. The words! Share house means shared bed. Short-order chef means tall-order lover. Drug courier means inject me here, yes, right here and now, come on, who cares what they think, what she thinks, they can arrest us for all I care, oh please won't you, you will won't you? Women need a reason to fuck but men only need a place eh? You won't? You arrogant arsehole! Those are the ones that go away with tight lips and dangerous fuck-you-nigger eyes. No sisterly cups of tea and vicarious intimacy for those ones, no.

Afterwards, we might laugh together about it — nervy, a bit too loud — but we laugh all the same. I tremble for him sometimes, my brother.

I looked on all this for years, and had my own fun in the shadows. Kept watching the queer boys' games, and the deadly seriousness of the flirting women. I saw people do terrible things in the name of love, saw civilisations thrown away for the sake of my brother's touch. If he wasn't innocent, neither was he very guilty. They came and adored him, and he let them. But then haven't the beautiful always got away with murder?

As for me, I kept my amateur status and thought myself immune — until you happened along. I looked one day and when you looked back I fell so hard and fast I hardly knew which way was up any more. It's too bad I'm married. It's too bad I can hardly speak at all.

You ring before you come over, a short dance of mild nothings on the phone, all the unsayables tucked into our (or at least my) back pockets. I don't know if you're coming alone. Whether you're bringing your lover. What to expect. I am pretty sure we both have unsayables, but as to what they are, aye, there's the rub. I'll show you yours if you — No. Stop it. I have to stop this right now.

I sing to myself about the house: *Because you're gorgeous, I'd do anything for you...*

I change my daggy jacket for a better one, and say nothing to my partner for fear that too much will leak out the sides of my sentences. Yes, I want to tell her, you can go now. This is a good time to leave. In literature, spouses are unobtrusive, ironically helpful. No, you should go and see him, he's expecting you. That sort of thing. In real life, partners hover, interrupt. Expect things. Sense nuances. Not that I'm having an affair, you understand. Not that I even want to.

And anyway it's not love we fall for, but the slick deceitful advertising. Passion. Romance. Lust. Dark strangers — please, a baker's dozen. Our egos lie quietly for a while, dormant on the floors of marriage, looking silently through the bars, and then one day they get up and stretch and yawn at the audience, showing those massive frightening teeth, and claws for ripping things apart. And if we're...is lucky the word? If the moment is right, someone sticks their head in your mouth, and it's up to us to decide. To bite down or not. That's where the advertising gets you, see. Top of the food chain. But once the head is in your mouth, you're on your own.

I go to the movies for badly needed Hollywood distraction. There's a gangsta with a gun to someone's head. She's snarling.

Just don't fuck wit me!

Oh, fuck with me whiteboy, fuck with me. I want to bite you scratch you suck you, I want to enslave you, I want to hurt you and make you cry out so I know you know I'm alive, I want to ride you and rub myself on you and oh yes, yes fuck with me do!

I talk with my friend about it, driving out of town on one of our lunatic expeditions, searching for other people who aren't there on a beach at midnight. Screaming names into the dark. Him, I tell her, I can't stop thinking about him, I know I'm married, I know it's stupid. She puts on a face, and says forget it, it's impossible. There isn't any answer. We keep yelling out the car window into the night, blundering down the sandy tracks. By the time we get home the moon has set and we are exhausted. We never found the ones we were looking for. They were somewhere else all along. Nothing was achieved. Do you hear me? Nothing.

But then I never say what I really want.

The Letter

Sally Morgan

The bus swayed back and forth making my tired old heart hurt even more.

Really, I wanted to cry, but no one cried on a bus. I glanced down sadly at the old biscuit tin sitting on my lap. Scotch Shortbreads, they weren't even her favourites, but she'd liked the colour of the tin so I'd given them to her.

I sighed and wiped away the tear that was beginning to creep down my cheek. She was gone, and I felt old and lonely and very disappointed.

My fingers traced around the lid of the old tin and slowly loosened it.

Inside was all she'd had to leave. A thin silvery necklace, some baby photos, her citizenship certificate, and the letter. I smiled when I remembered how it had taken her so long to write. She'd gone over and over every word. It was so important to her. We'd even joked about the day I would have to take it to Elaine. That day had come sooner than we both expected.

I've failed, I told myself as I lifted out the necklace. It'd been bought for Elaine's tenth birthday, but we hadn't known where to send it. Now we knew where Elaine lived but she didn't want the tin or anything in it.

I placed it back gently on top of the photo.

Elaine had said the baby in the photo wasn't her. She'd said it was all a silly mistake and she wished I'd stop pestering her.

It was the third time I'd been to see her and it looked like it would be the last. I picked up the letter. It was faded and worn. I opened it out carefully and read it again.

To my daughter Elaine,

I am writing in the hope that one day you will read this and understand. I suppose you don't want to know me because you think I deserted you. It wasn't like that. I want to tell you what it was like.

I was only seventeen when you were born at the Settlement. They all wanted to know who your father was, but I wouldn't tell. Of course he was a white man, you were so fair, but there was no love in his heart for you or me. I promised myself I would protect you. I wanted you to have a better life than me.

They took you away when I was twenty. Mr Neville from the Aborigines Protection Board said it was the best thing. He said that black mothers like me weren't allowed to keep babies like you. He didn't want you brought up as one of our people. I didn't want to let you go but I didn't have any choice. That was the law.

I started looking for you when I was thirty. No one would tell me where you'd gone. It was all a big secret. I heard they'd changed your last name, but I didn't know what your new name was. I went and saw Mr Neville and told him I wanted to visit you. That was when I found out that you'd been adopted by a white family. You thought you were white. Mr Neville said I'd only hurt you by trying to find you.

For a long time I tried to forget you, but how could I forget my own daughter? Sometimes I'd take out your baby photo and look at it and kiss your little face. I prayed that somehow you'd know you had a mother who loved you.

By the time I found you, you were grown up with a family of your own. I started sending you letters trying to reach you. I wanted to see you and my grandchildren, but you know all about that because you've sent all my letters back. I don't blame you and I don't hold any grudges, I understand. When you get this letter I will be gone, but you will have the special things in my tin. I hope that one day you will wonder who you really are and that you will make friends with our people because that's where you belong. Please be kind to the lady who gives you my tin, she's your own aunty.

From your loving Mother.

My hands were shaking as I folded the letter and placed it back in the tin. It was no use, I'd tried, but it was no use. Nellie had always been the strong one in our family, she'd never given up on anything. She'd always believed that one day Elaine would come home.

I pressed the lid down firmly and looked out the window at the passing road. It was good Nellie wasn't here now. I was glad she didn't know how things had turned out. Suddenly her voice seemed to whisper crossly in my ear. "You always give up too easy!"

"Do not," I said quietly. I didn't know what to do then. Nellie was right, that girl was our own flesh and blood, I couldn't let her go so easily. I looked down at the tin again and felt strangely better, almost happy. I'll make one last try, I thought to myself. I'll get a new envelope and mail it to her. She might just read it!

I was out in the yard when I heard the phone ring. I felt sure that by the time I got inside it would stop. It takes me a long while to get up the back steps these days. "Hello," I panted as I lifted the receiver. "Aunty Bessie?" "Who's this?" I asked in surprise. "It's Elaine." Elaine? I couldn't believe it! It'd been two months since I'd mailed the letter. "Is it really you Elaine?" I asked. "Yes, it's me. I want to talk to you. Can I come and see you?" "Ooh yes, any time."

"I'll be there tomorrow and Aunty...take care of yourself."

My hands shook as I placed the phone back on the hook.

Had I heard right? Had she really said, take care of yourself Aunty? I sat down quickly in the nearest chair and wiped my eyes.

"Well, why shouldn't I cry?" I said out loud to the empty room. "I'm not on the bus now!" Nellie felt very close to me just then. "Aah sister," I sighed. "Did you hear all that? Elaine will be here tomorrow?

"Did you hear that sister? Elaine's coming home."

Tired Sailor

from *Shark*

Bruce Pascoe

There was a place called Tired Sailor. A sea entrance backed by two estuarine lakes in the shape of a contented cow's stomach.

As you would expect with any well-established community, the village on the banks of the first lake was quiet, peaceful, happy and industrious, although none of those elements persisted for sufficient time to become tedious. They were interrupted by noise, conflict, death and laziness in sufficient regularity for the people to seek out ways of inhibiting the latter events and promoting the more enjoyable former. They were not sure if their efforts at resistance were successful, but as they were more often happy and safe than they were scared and dead, they persisted.

Of course they were black and of course they were killed. In their time the place had been called Weeaproinah which in their language meant, good fishing plenty yam milky tits fat baby warm dog sunny place sit down carve stick.

The first white people they saw appeared like ghosts under moving clouds and although the whites gave them a fat seal and only rooted a few women in return the people were anxious. None of their endeavours at performing increase rituals for their food and themselves had included clauses for the deterrence of white ghosts with black teeth whose bums always smelt of excreta.

The people at Weeaproinah hastily set about incorporating such measures into their ceremonies but, as they suspected in their hearts, it was to no avail. More smelly ghosts brought cows, boats, guns, shovels and influenza and the old days beside the lakes were gone.

The people of Weeaproinah were not keen to give up their oyster beds, wallaby pastures and yam paddocks but they were shot, poisoned and sickened. Some people stole a cow, speared a rapist, made irritating attempts to resume residence of their own houses but in the end they moved back into the swamps surrounding the western sides of the lakes. The last of them died sixty years after seeing her first white ghost.

The old village huts of Weeaproinah were knocked over and the new town of Tired Sailor rose. Houses, wharves and farms began to be tacked onto the lake's edge. It was a pleasant place. A row of small slab houses led down to the wharf and cow pastures velveted the rising ground behind them. Women brought in fruit trees, daffodils, lavender, honeysuckle and roses and the warm air of the estuary began to savour the new fragrances and mingle them with the old perfumes of pittosporum, bloodwood, bursaria and blueberry ash.

Old men sat on salt-bleached benches on the sunny side of their houses looking over the estuary and waiting for their sons to bring the boats across the sandbar at the entrance to the sea. The old men smoked their pipes and let the sun do those wondrous things it does to old bones. Tired Sailor, a lovely place for an old man to see out his last days.

Of course, it was these same old men who had shot and poisoned the black people, fucked their wives and drowned their children. But the old sailors reasoned that they had a king and an empire and the logical course for the peoples of empire was to become imperial and shift aside those who were not. Most of the pipe-smoking men in the sun regretted that Frazer had tied a child as bait to the bottom of a craypot and sent him into the deep still kicking and waving his arms. That was cruel and the others had always been wary of him since, but you couldn't have black men spearing white women and you couldn't have savages idling about on some of the best pasture land that God had created. It didn't make sense to the order of things as they and their forefathers knew it.

Patience, patience. Yes, it's black and white, starkly so, no shade, but there was no subtlety then, no room for it; the fight had to be won early or not at all and it was their duty as God's children to win it. God made them strong and righteous; they heralded from the flower of civilisation and it could not be imagined that God had not willed them, demanded them, to take the Bible, holiness, cholera and syphilis into all the Godless places of the world.

That's just how it was, the evidence is there and there's no purpose now in masticating the history for our babies' delicate digestion. Weeaproinah has become Tired Sailor. There is no more to be said.

Take today for instance. Here's Em Frazer rowing on the estuary. Yes, the great-granddaughter of Craypot Frazer. Now a lot of people think that Em is not the full quid. Two Lan Choo lids short of a milk jug. You don't get married, you spend twenty years looking after a mother with senile dementia and people think your soup bowl's cracked. But that's how it was. Em's mother thought she was a rabbit or something and always tried to piss and shit in the back yard. She'd lift her skirts and squat, twitching her nose. Em would go and get her, clean her up and put her back to bed. Em wasn't angry with her mother, the rabbit, just sad that this is how it had turned out and God had seen fit to make this her duty instead of having children or running the post office.

It had fallen to Em that, apart from the house, she also inherited her father's dinghy. All the Frazers' boats had been called *Pacific*. The old craypot murderer himself first painted the name on the clinker he built on the shores of this lake when he retired from the sealing business. The timber had been selected from the jungles at the further reaches of the river and sawn into planks in pits near the beach. All the boats since were basically the same and all were called *Pacific*. The clinkers were drawn up each night on the grass above high tide and there they rested aslant on their keels with *Pacific* on their bow and Tired Sailor on their stern.

So Em became the owner of *Pacific IV*. There would have been a neat boat per generation but *Pacific II* had been washed away in the great flood of 1909 and lost to the sea. Well, it wasn't actually lost. It washed up well down the coast three weeks later and Percy Mulgrew raced home and came back with two pots of paint and replaced *Pacific II* and Tired Sailor with *Mary Jane*, Swan's Reach. Mulgrew paid a carter £1 to load it on his dray and bring it into Swan's Reach via the back road so that people thought he'd acquired it elsewhere. Alec Campbell didn't think that because he'd seen the wheel ruts on the beach, but he settled for first use of Mulgrew's daughter. It's hard to like some people, although Colleen did love her baby and in time even found it not too unpleasant to wash Campbell's shirts and feed him stew. Accommodation. Most people on this part of the coast were practical and made the best use of what they found washed up on their beach.

And so was Em Frazer. She inherited *Pacific IV* and the bait licence that went with it. She was a worm pumper. At low tide, she'd row the dinghy out to the sandbanks either side of the estuary and pump worms and bass yabbies for the tourist fishermen.

She'd been doing this for many tides and sometimes in summer she was able to work two tides, morning and evening. On this particular day, however, she noticed something truly remarkable. Not a black panther escaped from the travelling circus (although her father had seen such a thing fifty years ago), not a man murdering his wife (although Tired Sailor's policeman had seen this twice in six years), not a lone shark chasing salmon over the bar in such shallow water that it had to belly hump across the sand (although she'd seen that herself several times), no, all of those things were remarkable, but Emily was transfixed by the sun rising and clouds slipping shadows across the intimate folding of the hills, into the places where, if you were God, you might splay your finger.

Emily let the bait pump dangle from her hand as she watched that slow caress and knew, what she'd always suspected, that there could be, even for one such as her, a benediction in love. He would come one day and take the bait pump from her hand and she would not be afraid. The man would not be Jesus but nor would it be the Rawleigh salesman or a squid fisherman. It would be a man who hardly spoke and therefore could not ask too much, could not ask for dinner at six or ironed pyjamas. She'd done that; she'd served as a nourisher and cleaner but her virgin body had remained her own and always would. The shadows of the sun had shown their intimation of intimacy and her heart warmed to the prospect of her vigil, waiting in certainty for him who would come with the hands shaped to the geography of her own undiscovered land.

The Serpent's Covenant

Alexis Wright

A nation chants, But we know your story already. The bells peal everywhere. Church bells calling the faithful to the tabernacle, where the gates of heaven will open, but not for the wicked. Calling innocent little black girls from a distant Aboriginal community where the white dove bearing an olive branch never lands. Little girls who come back home after church on Sunday, who look around themselves at the human fallout and announce matter of factly, Armageddon begins here.

The ancestral serpent, a creature larger than storm clouds, gathered itself on the horizon, came down from the stars laden with the vastness of creation. Perhaps it moved gracefully — if you had been watching with the eyes of a bird hovering in the sky far above the ground — its wet serpent's body glistening under an ancient sunlight. Perhaps it moved, those billions of years ago, with a speed unknown to man's measuring devices, to crawl on its heavy belly all around the wet clay soils in the Gulf of Carpentaria.

Picture the creative serpent scoring deep, scouring down through the slippery underground of the mud flats, leaving in its wake the thunderous sounds of tunnels collapsing to form deep sunken valleys. The sea water, following in its path, swarming in a frenzy of tidal waves, its colour changing from ocean blue to yellow mud, fills the serpent's swirling tracks to spread the mighty bending rivers across the vast plains of the Gulf country.

So the serpent travelled over stretches of marine plains, over the salt flats, through the salt dunes, past the mangrove forests and crawled inland. Then it went back to the sea. Further along the coastline it crawled inland once more and back again.

When it finished creating the many rivers on its travels, it created one last river, no larger or smaller than the others, a river that offers no apologies for its discontent to people who do not know it. This is where the giant serpent still lives, deep down under the ground in a vast network of limestone aquifers.

They say its being is porous, it permeates everything. It is all around in the atmosphere and is attached to the lives of the river people like skin.

In this tidal river its body takes in breaths of a size that is difficult to comprehend for a human mind no longer able to dream. Imagine the serpent's breathing rhythms to be the tide flowing inland, edging towards the spring waters nestled deeply in gorges of an ancient limestone plateau, covered with rattling grasses dried yellow from the prevailing winds. Then, with the outward breath, the tide turns and the serpent flows back to its own circulating mass of shallow waters — a giant water basin in a crook of the mainland geography, its sides separating it from the open sea. To catch this breath in the river you need the patience of one who can spend days doing nothing, waiting under the river gum where those up to no good type mission-breed kids accidentally hanged Cry-baby Sally.

The inside knowledge about this river and coastal region is the traditional knowledge of Aboriginal law handed down through the ages since time began. Otherwise how would one know where to look for the hidden underwater courses in the vast flooding mudplains, full of serpents and fish in the monsoon season of summer? Can someone who did not grow up in a place that is sometimes under water, sometimes bone-dry, know when the trade winds blowing off the southern and northern hemispheres will merge in summer? Know the moment of climatic change better than they know themselves? Can they fish in the yellow-coloured monsoonal runoff, its sheets of deep waters pouring into the wide rivers that have swollen over its banks to fill the vast plains with flood waters? In the meantime, the cyclones linger and regroup, the rain never stops pouring, but the fat fish are abundant.

It takes a particular kind of knowledge to go with the river, whatever its mood. It is about there being no difference between you and the movement of water. The river spurns human endeavour in one dramatic gesture, like jilting a lover never really known, as it did to the frontier town built on its banks in the hectic heyday of colonial vigour.

In one moment, during one wet season early in the century, the town lost its harbour waters when the river simply decided to change course. Just like that. The waterless port, built to serve the shipping trade of the northern hinterland, survives with nothing much to do. Meanwhile, its citizens continue a dialogue with themselves, passed down through the generations, on why the town should continue to exist. They stayed on to safeguard the northern coastline from the imminent invasion of the Yellow Peril. (A dreadful vision, a long yellow streak marching behind an arrowhead pointing straight for Port D'Arcy). But then, when the Yellow Peril did not invade, everyone had a good look around and found a more immediate concern. It meant the town still had to be vigilant. Duty did not fall on one or two; duty was everybody's business — to keep a good eye out and give voice to a testimonial far beyond personal experience. It was regarded as maintaining the decent society of the nation as a whole — to comment on the state of their local Blacks.

Norm Phantom was an old tribal man from the dense prickle bush scrub on the edge of town. He'd lived all of his life amidst thickets of closely growing slender plants with barely anything for leaves, that never gave an ant an inch of shelter under a thousand of its thorny branches. This foreign infestation on the edge of Port D'Arcy had been growing long before anyone in the Phantom family could remember. They had lived out there next to the smell of the town tip since the day Norm was born. All choked up, living piled up together in trash humpies made of tin, cloth and plastic too, salvaged from the rubbish dump. The descendants of the pioneer families, who claimed ownership of the town, said the Aboriginal was really not part of the town at all (conceding that they worked the dunny cart in the old days, carted the rubbish and swept the street). Furthermore, they said, the Aboriginal was dumped here by the pastoralists. Refused to pay the blackfella equal wages, even when the law came in. Right on the edge of somebody else's town, didn't they?

But the prickle bush was from the time just before the motor car, when goods and chattels came up by camel train with the old Afghan brothers, Abdullah and Abdul. They disappeared one year along the track called the lifeline, which connected north to south. After much time had passed, the jokes came about Afghans being shifty dogs, dodgy dogs, murdering dogs and — unreliable. When the cupboards turned bare, the town talk finally crystallised into one sensible realisation that very likely the camel men were never coming back; then everyone in town assumed they had died. A few of the Christian-minded, capitalising on the town's gross lack of decency, sniffed: Well! That ought to teach you now, won't it? But no one else thought so, because by then the grog and the tucker were being freighted up by mail truck, which everyone thought was a more convenient method of road transport by any stretch of the imagination.

One cloud-covered night, the camels finally turned up in Port D'Arcy, jingling and a-jangling, their foreign bells swaying around their necks, vespers on such a still night. At once, the residents woke in childlike fright, sitting straight up in their beds, wide eyes seeing dark figures moving in their pitch-black bedrooms, same time reckoning it was ghosts with an Afghan smell. True God, just came straight in, levitating, taking over, helping themselves, walking around people's homes with no mind youse, not one shred of good manners whatsoever. That was the trouble with new Australians — even dead ones had no manners. Unnaturalised. Really un-Australian. Neighbours passed the buck in mind-talk. You shoulda sent out a search party. What a relief when dawn came and everyone could see for themselves it was just poor old Abdullah and Abdul's camels.

Over the following days no one thought to capture the animals and retrieve the rotting pack saddles. The townsfolk had a deeply felt aversion to touching the belongings of dark-skinned foreigners — and their animals. So the camels just wandered around at will, all covered with yaws from the rotting packs of foodstuffs — flour, sugar, grain that had sprouted and died, still strapped over and hanging off their backs — until something had to be done. After being hounded, stoned and whipped for several hours by their pursuers on foot and horseback, the camels were eventually moved out over the claypans and shot. It's there in the archival records, written with a thick nib by a heavy-handed municipal clerk: Camels removed.

The prickle bush mob say that Norm could grab hold of the river in his mind. Just as his father's fathers had before him. His ancestors were the river people since before time began. Norm was like ebbing water, he came and went on the flowing waters of the river, right out to the sea. He stayed away on the water as long as he pleased. So it seemed to everyone who talked about him. He knew fish and he was on friendly terms with gropers, the giant cod fish of the Gulf sea that swam in schools of fifty or more; they'd move right up the river, following his boat in for company. The old people say the groper lives for hundreds of years, and maybe Norm would too. They said he knew as much about the stars as he did about the water. The prickle bush mob said he had always chased the constellations: We watched him as a little boy running off into the night trying to catch stars. They were certain he knew the secret of getting there. They thought he went right up to the stars in the company of the groper fish when it stormed at sea, when the sea and the sky became one. How you do that? was the question everyone asked. The water doesn't worry me, Norm answered simply, although he knew there was more to it than that. When his mind went for a walk, his body followed.

Everyone at Port D'Arcy was used to the sight of Norm's jeep driving north to meet up with the river's edge. It was the only vehicle Norm ever owned. Always the small tinnie boat — full of dints, a stray bullet hole or two — strapped onto the roof. A vessel purchased with cross-country road transport in mind, much more than water safety.

They say he knew those deep muddy waters better than the big salties that got tangled up in the nets in the middle of the night. Glassy-eyed monsters that came over the side of his tiny craft looking for action, angry jaws charging for a fight in the swamping boat, snapping in full flight, water splashing up into a storm with the swishing and thrashing of an angry tail against the side of the boat. People like to remember Norm saying in a nonchalant fashion, faking a thoroughly modern American accent, that those snapping jaws meant diddly squat to him. Must have remembered seeing it on TV.

If the truth be known, he moved like a hopping hare, fumbling for what seemed ages to find the gun. Norm ended hundreds of reptilian lives this way, his gun pointing all over the place in a turmoil of water and thick leather crankiness until he made a direct hit between eyes caught in an instant of moonlight. The rifle he claimed to have won in a fight — according to local gossip, while screaming for the Lord to buy him a Mercedes Benz.

Curiously, in this otherwise long-memoried population of about three hundred people, no living soul remembered what the port had looked like. No picture could be put on display in a showcase at the museum of scarce memorabilia, because no one at the time of the heyday had thought it was worthwhile to take a photo. But it was clear that everybody knew that this was Norm's river.

One day, someone was languishing in a laconic stupor in the wet season build up, waiting for the rain to come. They lay flat-out like a corpse on the bare linoleum floor in the hallway of a house exactly like the one next door, capturing in a long sigh of appreciation the northern sea breeze that came waltzing straight over twenty-five kilometres of mud flats. It whistled its arrival through the front door and slammed the back door shut on its way out. All of a sudden this someone thought of changing the name of the river. To Norm.

And, in a town where change never came easy, it came to be.

There was a celebration by the local shire council. The occasion was the anniversary of the port's first one hundred years. It coincided with a spate of unusual happenings that occurred under a short-lived era of Aboriginal domination of the council. Harmless coercing of the natives, the social planners hummed, anxious to make deals happen before the impending mining boom. During this honeymoon period those Aboriginal people who took the plunge to be councillors wisely used their time in public office to pursue scraps of personal gain for their own families living amidst the muck of third world poverty. Meaningful coexistence could now accommodate almost any request whatsoever, including changing a river's name to Norm.

All this was part and parcel of the excitement over the first multinational mining company coming into the region. Numerous short-lived profiteering schemes were concocted for the locals to serve the company's own pre-determined interests as they set about pillaging the region's treasure trove. A publicly touted curve of an underground range embedded with rich mineralisation.

The elaborate white linen ceremony attracted the southern politicians. A bunch of fly-by-nighters, who flew in for the day. And as they rolled out the welcome smile, some of the locals whispered unmentionable insults behind the backs of their very important visitors. Others, who liked the sound of their own voices, attacked the politicians straight out with a diatribe of insults. The crowd picked up bits wafting in the wind gusts: Youse are always cowering down on the ground ... Are youse the runt of the Australian political litter or something? ... Yah! falling over yaselves to any foreign investor flocking up the steps of State Parliament, knocking on the big door and kind of smelling like money...

The politicians and mining executives, who sponsored the event with a more or less open cheque, mingled uncomfortably with the crowd. They pushed themselves up against old Norm for a photo opportunity, grinning before the members of the media circus who had jockeyed for a free ride on the official executive jets to attend the event.

But the proceedings had to be rushed through by the compere, a popular radio personality from a neighbouring shire. Everything got ruined by a normal sort of dust storm thundering in from the south. A thick wall of red dust mingled with all manner of crunched vegetation and plastic shopping bags that it had gathered up in its path damaged all of the cut sandwiches, among other things. Fingers, toes, eyes, ears, noses and lips became covered with a powdery layer of grit. Fidget-prone adults panicked, running for cover along with their red and green cordial-stained screaming children.

Then came a violent electrical storm and the rain ruined the day anyway — just as the town's sceptics had said it would. A taut occasion, despite these dramatic interventions. But enough time had transpired for the now-deposed State Premier to complete the ceremony of officially changing the name of the river from that of a long-deceased imperial queen to Norm's River. Traditional people who gathered up for the event mumbled, Ngabarn, Ngabarn, Mandagi, and so did Norm in a very loud and sour-sounding voice over the loud-speaker in his extremely short thank-you address. Those who knew a fruit salad full of abuse in the local language knew he was not saying Thank you! Thank you! and belly-laughed themselves silly because the river only had one name from the beginning of time. It was called Wangala.

It was a funny thing about the river. Everybody wanted to have a part of it, perhaps hoping to be a little bit like Norm. Anybody and everybody thought they might ride the river like some legendary buckjumping wild horse called Diesel or Gidgee or Mulga. More and more people started travelling up the northern coastline over the rough roads of the Gulf on long weekends. They'd haul up and launch flash fishing boats called *Donna*, *Stella* and *Trixie* straight over the side into the yellow river. Bright coloured, high-powered boats, bought with top dollar gained from doing stretch shifts two kilometres underground, where they hauled up rich ores scraped from the mother lode embedded in sequences of rock that look like the growth rings of a powerful ancient being.

And on the water they would cast a line here, a line there, with state-of-the-art fishing tackle, but no knowledge of the way of the river. Nothing was thought about it. What mattered was that there were a considerable number of people living in the region now, with the great influx of mine workers who had nothing to do on their days off. The little boom and die towns were fast and modern, in a barely disguised country-and-western style commercial frontierism. Meanwhile, more new mines became established in the region with little regard to what was anyone's say-so.

When the mining stopped, neither Norm Phantom and his family nor his family's relations, past or present, rated a mention in the official version of the region's history. There was no tangible evidence of their existence. Even in Uncle Micky's collection of bullet cartridges.

Micky had lived with a metal detector for God knows how long. He said he had a fever which drove him on because he would never know when he picked up the last piece of evidence — all of those forty-fours, thirty-thirtys, three-o-threes, twelve gauges — all kinds of cartridges used in the massacre of the local tribes. He had maps, names of witnesses, details, the lot. A walking encyclopaedia. Now his voice lives on in the great archive of cassettes which he left for the war trials he predicted would happen one day. But no tourists go to Micky's museum. Maybe because it was built in the wrong spot. But that's fighting for you. Fighting, fighting all the time for a bit of land and a little bit of recognition.

Then all the old mines, old mining equipment, old miners, old miners' huts, anything to do with mining was packaged in a mishmash and marketed on gloss as the ultimate local tourist attraction. The shiny tourist brochures celebrating selected historical sites and museums were there to grab you from across the room of airports, hotels and motels, or from the rack of any tourist or travel centre selling the highlights of the region.

But this was not vaudeville. Wars were fought here. If you had your patch destroyed, you'd be screaming too. The serpent's covenant permeates everything, even the little black girls with hair combed back off their faces and bobby-pinned neatly for church, listening quietly to the nation that claims to know everything except the exact date their world will end. Then, almost whispering, they shyly ask if the weather had been forecast correctly today?

If you are someone who visits old cemeteries, wait awhile if you visit the water people. The old Gulf Country men and women who took our besieged memories to the grave might just climb out of the mud and tell you the real story of what happened here.

Maori

Aotearoa
(New Zealand)

It Used to be Green Once

Patricia Grace

We were all ashamed of our mother. Our mother always did things to shame us. Like putting red darns in our clothes, and cutting up old swimming togs and making two — girl's togs from the top half for my sister, and boy's togs from the bottom half for my brother. Peti and Raana both cried when Mum made them take the togs to school. Peti sat down on the road by our gate and yelled out she wasn't going to school. She wasn't going swimming. I didn't blame my sister because the togs were thirty-eight chest and Peti was only ten.

But Mum knew how to get her up off the road. She yelled loudly, "Get up off that road, my girl. There's nothing wrong with those togs. I didn't have any togs when I was a kid and I had to swim in my nothings. Get up off your backside and get to school." Mum's got a loud voice and she knew how to shame us. We all dragged Peti up off the road before our mates came along and heard Mum. We pushed Peti into the school bus so Mum wouldn't come yelling up the drive.

We never minded our holey fruit at first. Dad used to pick up the cases of over-ripe apples or pears from town that he got cheap. Mum would dig out the rotten bits, and then give them to us to take for play-lunch. We didn't notice much at first, not until Reweti from down the road yelled out to us one morning, "Hey you fullas. Who shot your pears?" We didn't have anywhere to hide our lunch because we weren't allowed schoolbags until we got to high school. Mum said she wasn't buying fourteen schoolbags. When we went to high school we could have shoes too. The whole lot of us gave Reweti a good hiding after school.

However, this story is mainly about the car, and about Mum and how she shamed us all the time. The shame of rainbow darns and cut-up togs and holey fruit was nothing to what we suffered because of the car. Uncle Raz gave us the car because he couldn't fix it up any more, and he'd been fined because he lived in Auckland. He gave the car to Dad so we could drive our cream cans up to the road instead of pushing them up by wheelbarrow.

It didn't matter about the car not having brakes, because the drive from our cowshed goes down in a dip then up to the gate. Put the car in its first gear, run it down from the shed, pick up a bit of speed, up the other side, turn it round by the cream stand so that it's pointing down the drive again, foot off the accelerator and slam on the handbrake. Dad pegged a board there to make sure it stopped. Then when we'd lifted the cans out onto the stand, he'd back up a little and slide off down the drive — with all of us throwing ourselves in over the sides as if it were a dinghy that had just been pushed out into the sea.

The car had been red once, because you could still see some patches of red paint here and there. And it used to have a top too, that you could put down or up. Our uncle told us that when he gave it to Dad. We were all proud about the car having had a top once. Some of the younger kids skited to their mates about our convertible and its top that went up and down. But that was before our mother started shaming us by driving the car to the shop.

We growled at Mum and we cried but it made no difference. "You kids always howl when I tell you to get our shopping," she said.

"We'll get it, Mum. We won't cry."

"We won't cry, Mum. We'll carry the sack of potatoes."

"And the flour."

"And the bag of sugar."

"And the tin of treacle."

"We'll do the shopping, Mum."

But Mum would say, "Never mind. I'll do it myself." And after that she wouldn't listen anymore.

How we hated Wednesdays. We always tried to be sick on Wednesdays, or to miss the bus. But Mum would be up early yelling at us to get out of bed. If we didn't get up when we were told she'd drag us out and pull down our pyjama pants and set our bums on the cold lino. Mum was cruel to us.

Whoever was helping with the milking had to be back quickly from the shed for breakfast, and we'd all have to rush through our kai and get to school. Wednesday was Mum's day for shopping.

As soon as she had everything tidy she'd change into her good purple dress that she'd made from a Japanese bedspread, pull on her floppy brimmed blue sunhat and her slippers and galoshes, and go out and start up the car.

We tried everything to stop her shaming us all.

"You've got no licence Mum."

"What do I want a licence for? I can drive can't I? I don't need the proof."

"You got no warrant."

"Warrant? What's warrant?"

"The traffic man'll get you Mum."

"That rat. He won't come near me after what he did to my niece. I'll hit 'im right over his smart head with a bag of riwais and I'll hit him somewhere else as well."

We never could win an argument with Mum.

Off she'd go on a Wednesday morning, and once out on the road she'd start tooting the horn. This didn't sound like a horn at all but more like a flock of ducks coming in for a feed. The reason for the horn was to let all her mates and relations along the way know she was coming. And as she passed each one's house, if they wanted anything they'd have to run out and call it out loud. Mum couldn't stop because of not having any brakes. "E Kiri," each would call. "Mauria mai he riwai," if they wanted spuds; "Mauria mai he paraoa," if they wanted bread. "Mauria mai he tarau, penei te kaita," hand spread to show the size of the pants they wanted Mum to get. She would call out to each one and wave to them to show she'd understood. And when she neared the store she'd switch the motor off, run into the kerbing and pull on the handbrake. I don't know how she remembered all the things she had to buy — I only know that by the time she'd finished every space in the car was filled and it was a squeeze for her to get into the driver's seat. But she had everything there, all ready to throw out on the way back.

As soon as she'd left the store she'd begin hooting again, to let the whole district know she was on her way. Everybody would be out on the road to get their shopping thrown at them, or just to watch our mother go chuffing past. We always hid if we heard her coming.

The first time Mum's car and the school bus met was when they were both approaching a one-way bridge from opposite directions. We had to ask the driver to stop and give way to Mum because she had no brakes. We were all ashamed. But everyone soon got to know Mum and her car. And you know, Mum never had an accident in her car, except for once when she threw a side of mutton out to Uncle Peta and it knocked him over and broke his leg.

After a while we started walking home from school on Wednesdays to give Mum a good chance of getting home before us, and so we wouldn't be in the bus when it had to stop and let her past. The boys didn't like having to walk home, but we girls didn't mind because Mr Hadley walked home too. He was a new teacher at our school and he stayed not far from where we lived. We girls thought he was really neat.

But one day, it had to happen. When I heard the honking and tooting behind me I wished a hole would appear in the ground and that I would fall in it and disappear for ever. As Mum came near she started smiling and waving and yelling her head off. "Anyone wants a ride," she yelled, "they'll have to run and jump in."

We all turned our heads the other way and hoped Mr Hadley wouldn't notice the car with our mother in it, and her yelling and tooting, and the brim of her hat jumping up and down. But instead, Mr Hadley took off after the car and leapt in over the back seat on top of the shopping. Oh the shame.

But then one day something happened that changed everything. We arrived home to find Dad in his best clothes, walking round and grinning, and not doing anything like getting the cows in, or mending a gate, or digging a drain. We said, "What are you laughing at, Dad? What are you dressed up for? Hey Mum, what's the matter with Dad?"

"Your dad's a rich man," she said. "Your dad, he's just won ten thousand pounds in a lottery."

At first we couldn't believe it. We couldn't believe it. Then we all began running round and laughing and yelling and hugging Dad and Mum. "We can have shoes and bags," we said. "New clothes and swimming togs, and proper apples and pears." Then do you know what Dad said? Dad said, "Mum can have a new car." This really astounded and amazed us. We went numb with excitement for five minutes then began hooting and shouting again, and knocking Mum over.

"A new car!"

"A new car?"

"Get us a Packard, Mum."

"Or a De Soto. Yes, yes."

Get this, get that...

Well, Mum bought a big shiny green Chevrolet, and Dad got a new cowshed with everything modernised and water gushing everywhere. We all got our new clothes — shoes, bags, togs — and we even started taking posh lunches to school. Sandwiches cut in triangles, bottles of cordial, crisp apples and pears, and yellow bananas.

And somehow all of us kids changed. We started acting like we were somebody instead of ordinary like before. We used to whine at Dad for money to spend, and he'd always give it to us. Every week we'd nag Mum into taking us to the pictures, or if she was tired we'd go ourselves by taxi. We got flash bedspreads and a piano and we really thought we were neat.

As for the old car — we made Dad take it to the dump. We never wanted to see it again. We all cheered when he took it away, except for Mum. Mum stayed inside where she couldn't watch, but we all stood outside and cheered.

We all changed, as though we were really somebody, but there was one thing I noticed. Mum didn't change at all, and neither did Dad. Mum had a new car all right, and a couple of new dresses, and a new pair of galoshes to put over her slippers. And Dad had a new modern milking shed and a tractor, and some other gadgets for the farm. But Mum and Dad didn't change. They were the same as always.

Mum still went shopping every Wednesday. But instead of having to do all the shopping herself, she was able to take all her friends and relations with her. She had to start out earlier so she'd have time to pick everyone up on the way. How angry we used to be when Mum went past with her same old sunhat and her heap of friends and relations, and them all waving and calling out to us.

Mum sometimes forgot the new car had brakes, especially when she was approaching the old bridge and we were coming the opposite way in the school bus. She would start tooting and the bus would have to pull over and let her through. That's when all our aunties and uncles and friends would start waving and calling out. But some of them couldn't wave because they were too squashed by people and shopping, they'd just yell. How shaming.

There were always ropes everywhere over Mum's new car holding bags of things and shovel handles to the roof and sides. The boot was always hanging open because it was too full to close — things used to drop out onto the road all the time. And the new car — it used to be green once, because if you look closely you can still see some patches of green paint here and there.

Ngati Kangaru

Patricia Grace

Billy was laughing his head off reading the history of the New Zealand Company, har, har, har, har.

It was since he'd been made redundant from Mitre 10 that he'd been doing all this reading. Billy and Makere had four children, one who had recently qualified as a lawyer but was out of work, one in her final year at university, and two at secondary school. These kids ate like elephants. Makere's job as a checkout operator for New World didn't bring in much money and she thought Billy should be out looking for another job instead of sitting on his backside all day reading and laughing.

The book belonged to Rena, whose full given names were Erena Meretiana. She wanted the book back so she could work on her assignment. Billy had a grip on it.

Har, har, these Wakefields were real crooks. That's what delighted Billy. He admired them, and at the beginning of his reading had been distracted for some minutes while he reflected on that first one, EG Wakefield, sitting in the clink studying up on colonisation. Then by the time of his release, EG had the edge on all those lords, barons, MPs, lawyers and so forth. Knew more about colonisation than they did, haaar.

However, Billy wasn't too impressed with the reason for EG's incarceration. Abducting an heiress? Jeepers! Billy preferred more normal, more cunning crookery, something funnier — like lying, cheating and stealing.

So in that regard he wasn't disappointed as he read on, blobbed out in front of the two-bar heater that was expensive to run, Makere reminded him. Yes, initial disappointment left him the more he progressed in his reading. Out-and-out crooks, liars, cheats and thieves, these Wakefields. He felt inspired.

What he tried to explain to Makere was that he wasn't just spending his time idly while he sat there reading. He was learning a few things from EG, WW, Jerningham, Arthur and Co., that would eventually be of benefit to him as well as to the whole family. He knew it in his bones.

"Listen to this," he'd say, as Makere walked in the door on feet that during the course of the day had grown and puffed out over the tops of her shoes. And he'd attempt to interest her with excerpts from what he'd read. "'The Wakefields' plan was based on the assumption that vast areas — if possible, every acre — of New Zealand would be bought for a trifle, the real payment to the people of the land being their "civilising"...' Hee hee, that's crafty. They called it 'high and holy work'.

"And here. There was this 'exceptional law' written about in one of EG's anonymous publications, where chiefs sold a heap of land for a few bob and received a section 'in the midst of emigrants' in return. But har, har, the chiefs weren't allowed to live on this land until they had 'learned to estimate its value'. Goodby-ee, don't cry-ee. It was held in reserve waiting for the old fellas to be brainy enough to know what to do with it.

"Then there was this 'adopt-a-chief scheme', a bit like the 'dial-a-kaumatua' scheme that they have today where you bend some old bloke's ear for an hour or two, let him say a few wise words and get him to do the old rubber-stamp trick, hee, hee. Put him up in a flash hotel and give him a ride in an aeroplane then you've consulted with every iwi throughout Aotearoa, havintcha? Well, 'adopt-a-chief' was a bit the same except the prizes were different. They gave out coats of arms, lessons in manners and how to mind your p's and q's, that sort of stuff. I like it. You could do anything as long as you had a 'worthy cause'," and Billy would become pensive. "A worthy cause. Orl yew need is a werthy caws."

On the same day that Billy finished reading the book he found his worthy cause. He had switched on television to watch Te Karere, when the face of his first cousin Hiko, who lived in Poi Hakena, Australia, came onto the screen.

The first shots showed Hiko speaking to a large rally of Maori people in Sydney who had formed a group called Te Hokinga ki Aotearoa. This group was in the initial stages of planning for a mass return of Maori to their homeland.

In the interview that followed, Hiko explained that there was disillusionment among Maori people with life in Australia and that they now wanted to return to New Zealand. Even the young people who had been born in Australia, who may never have seen Aotearoa, were showing an interest in their ancestral home. The group included three or four millionaires, along with others who had made it big in Oz , as well as those on the bones of their arses — or that's how Billy translated into English what Hiko had said in Maori, to Hana and Gavin. These two were Hana Angeline and Gavin Rutene, the secondary schoolers, who had left their homework to come and gog at their uncle on television.

Hiko went on to describe what planning would be involved in the first stage of The Return, because this transfer of one hundred families was the first stage only. The ultimate plan was to return all Maori people living in Australia to Aotearoa, iwi by iwi. But the groups didn't want to come home to nothing, was what Hiko was careful to explain. They intended all groups to be well housed and financed on their return, and discussions and decisions on how to make it all happen were in progress. Billy's ears prickled when Hiko began to speak of the need for land, homes, employment and business ventures. "'Possess yourselves of the soil'," he muttered, "'and you are secure'."

Ten minutes later he was on the phone to Hiko.

By the time the others returned — Makere from work, Tu from job-hunting and Rena from varsity — Billy and the two children had formed a company, composed a rap, cleared a performance space in front of the dead fireplace, put their caps on backwards and practised up to performance standard:

First you go and form a Co.
Make up lies and advertise
Buy for a trifle the land you want
For Jew's harps, nightcaps
Mirrors and beads

Sign here sign there
So we can steal
And bring home cuzzies
To their "Parent Isle"

Draw up allotments on a map
No need to buy just occupy
Rename the places you now own
And don't let titles get you down
For blankets, fish hooks, axes and guns
Umbrellas, sealing wax, pots and clothes

Sign here, sign there
So we can steal
And bring home cuzzies
To their "Parent Isle"

Bought for a trifle sold for a bomb
Homes for your rellies
And dollars in the bank
Bought for a trifle sold for a bomb
Homes for your rellies
And dollars in the bank

Ksss Aue. Aue,
Hi.

Billy, Hana and Gavin bowed to Makere, Tu and Rena. "You are looking at a new company," Billy said, "which from henceforward (his vocabulary had taken on some curiosities since he had begun reading histories) will be known as Te Kamupene o Te Hokinga Mai."

"Tell Te Kamupene o Te Hokinga Mai to cough up for the mortgage," said Makere, disappearing offstage with her shoes in her hand.

"So all we need," said Billy to Makere, later in the evening, "is a vast area of land 'as far as the eye can see'."

"Is that all?" said Makere.

"Of 'delightful climate' and 'rich soil' that is 'well watered and coastal'. Of course it'll need houses on it too, the best sort of houses, luxury style."

"Like at Claire Vista," said Makere. Billy jumped out of his chair and his eyes jumped out, "Brilliant, Ma, brilliant." He planted a kiss on her unimpressed cheek and went scrabbling in a drawer for pen and paper so that he could write to Hiko.

...the obvious place for the first settlement of Ngati Kangaru, it being "commodious and attractive". But more importantly, as you know, Claire Vista is the old stamping ground of our iwi that was confiscated at the end of last century, and is now a luxury holiday resort. Couldn't be apter. We must time the arrival of our people for late autumn when the holidaymakers have all left. I'll take a trip up there on Saturday and get a few snaps, which I'll send. Then I'll draw up a plan and we can do our purchases. Between us we should be able to see everyone home and housed by June next year. Timing your arrival will be vital. I suggest you book flights well in advance so that you all arrive at once. We will charter buses to take you to your destination and when you arrive we will hold the official welcome-home ceremony and see you all settled into your new homes.

The next weekend he packed the company photographer with her camera and the company secretary with his notebook and biro, into the car. He, the company manager, got in behind the wheel and they set out for Claire Vista.

At the top of the last rise, before going down into Claire Vista, Billy stopped the car. While he was filling the radiator, he told Hana to take a few shots. And to Gavin he said, "Have a good look, son, and write down what the eye can see."

"On either side of where we're stopped," wrote Gavin, "there's hills and natral vejetation. There's this long road down on to this flat land that's all covered in houses and parks. There's this long, straight beach on the left side and the other side has lots of small beaches. There's this airport for lite planes and a red windsock showing hardly any wind. One little plane is just taking off. There's boats coming and going on the water as far as the I can see, and there's these two islands, one like a sitting dog and one like a duck."

Their next stop was at the Claire Vista Information Centre, where they picked up street maps and brochures, after which they did a systematic tour of the streets, stopping every now and again to take photographs and notes.

"So what do I do?" asked Tu, who had just been made legal advisor of the company. He was Tuakana Petera and this was his first employment.

"Get parchments ready for signing," said Billy.

"Do you mean deeds of title?"

"That's it," said Billy. Then to Rena, the company's new researcher, he said, "Delve into the histories and see what you can come up with for new brochures. Start by interviewing Nanny."

"I've got exams in two weeks I'll have you know."

"After that will do."

The next day Billy wrote to Hiko to say that deeds of title were being prepared and requested that each of the families send two thousand dollars for working capital. He told him that a further thousand dollars would be required on settlement. "For four thousand bucks you'll get a posh house with boat, by the sea, where there are recreation parks, and amenities, anchorage and launching ramps, and a town with good shopping, only twenty minutes away. Also it's a good place to set up businesses for those who don't want to fish all the time.

"Once the deeds of sale have been made up for each property I'll get the signatures on them and then they'll be ready. I'll also prepare a map of the places, each place to be numbered, and when all the first payments have been made you can hold a lottery where subscribers' tickets are put into 'tin boxes'. Then you can have ceremonies where the names and numbers will be drawn out by a 'beautiful boy'. This is a method that has been used very successfully in the past, according to my information.

"Tomorrow we're going out to buy Jew's harps, muskets, blankets (or such like) as exchange for those who sign the parchments."

"You'll have a hundred families all living in one house, I suppose," said Makere, "because that's all you'll get with four thousand dollars a family."

"'Possess yourselves of the homes'," said Billy.

"What's that supposed to mean?"

"It's a 'wasteland'. They're waste homes. They're all unoccupied. Why have houses unoccupied when there are people wanting to occupy them?"

"Bullshit. Hana and Gav didn't say the homes were unoccupied."

"That's because it's summertime. End of March everyone's gone and there are good homes going to waste. 'Reclaiming and cultivating a moral wilderness', that's what we're doing, 'serving to the highest degree', that's what we're on about, 'according to a deliberate and methodical plan'."

"Doesn't mean you can just walk in and take over."

"Not unless we get all the locks changed."

By the end of summer the money was coming in and Billy had all the deeds of sale printed, ready for signing. Makere thought he was loopy thinking that all these rich wallahs would sign their holiday homes away.

"Not *them*," Billy said. "You don't get *them* to sign. You get other people. That's how it was done before. Give out pressies — tobacco, biscuits, pipes, that sort of thing, so that they, whoever they are, will mark the parchments."

Makere was starting to get the hang of it, but she huffed all the same.

"Now I'm going out to get us a van," Billy said. "Then we'll buy the trifles. After that, tomorrow and the next day, we'll go and round up some derros to do the signing."

It took a week to get the signatures, and during that time Billy and the kids handed out — to park benchers in ten different parts of the city — one hundred bottles of whiskey, one hundred packets of hot pies and one hundred old overcoats.

"What do you want our signatures for?" they asked.

"Deeds of sale for a hundred properties up in Claire Vista," Billy said.

"The only Claire Vistas we've got is where our bums hit the benches."

"Well, look here." Billy showed them the maps with allotments marked out on them and they were interested and pleased. "Waste homes," Billy explained. "All these fellas have got plenty of other houses all over the place, but they're simple people who know nothing about how to fully utilise their properties and they can 'scarcely cultivate the earth'. But who knows they might have a 'peculiar aptitude for being improved'. It's 'high and holy work', this."

"Too right. Go for it," the geezers said. Billy and the kids did their rap for them and moved on, pleased with progress.

In fact everything went so well that there was nothing much left to do after that. When he wrote to Hiko, Billy recommended that settlement to Claire Vista be speeded up. "We could start working on places for the next hundred families now and have all preparations done in two months. I think we should make an overall target of one hundred families catered for every two months over the next ten months. That means in March we get our first hundred families home, then another lot in May, July, September, November. By November we'll have five hundred Ngati Kangaru families, i.e., about four thousand people, settled before the holiday season. We'll bring in a few extra families from here (including ourselves) and that means that every property in Claire Vista will have new owners. If the Te Karere news crew comes over there again," he wrote, "make sure to tell them not to give our news to any other language. Hey, Bro, let's just tap the sides of our noses with a little tip of finger. Keep it all nod nod, wink wink, for a while."

On the fifth of November there was a big welcome-home ceremony, with speeches and food and fireworks at the Claire Vista hall, which had been renamed Te Whare Ngahau o Ngati Kangaru. At the same time Claire Vista was given back its former name of Ikanui and discussions took place regarding the renaming of streets, parks, boulevards, avenues, courts, dells and glens after its reclaimers.

By the time the former occupants began arriving in mid-December, all the signs in the old Claire Vista had been changed and the new families were established in their new homes. It was a lovely, soft and green life at that time of the year. One in which you could stand barefooted on grass or sand in your shorts and shirt and roll your eyes round. You could slide your boat down the ramp, cruise about, toss the anchor over and put your feet up, fish, pull your hat down. Whatever.

On the day that the first of the holidaymakers arrived at 6 Ara Hakena, with their bags and holiday outfits, Christmas presents, CDs, six-packs, cartons of groceries, snorkels, lilos and things, the man and woman and two sub-teenagers were met by Mere and Jim Hakena, their three children, Jim's parents and a quickly gathering crowd of neighbours.

At first, Ruby and Gregory in their cotton co-ordinates, and Alister with his school friend in their stonewash jeans, apricot and applegreen tees, and noses zinked pink and orange, thought they could've come to the wrong house, especially since its address seemed to have changed and the neighbours were different.

But how could it be the wrong house? It was the same windowy place in stained weatherboard, designed to suit its tree environment and its rocky outlook. There was the new skylit extension and glazed brick barbecue. Peach tree with a few green ones. In the drive in front of the underhouse garage they could see the spanking blue boat with *Sea Urchin* in cursive along its prow. The only difference was that the boat was hitched to a green Landcruiser instead of to a red Range Rover.

"That's our boat," said Ruby.

"I doubt it," said Mere and Jim together, folding their arms in unison.

"He paid good money for that," a similarly folded-armed neighbour said. "It wasn't much but it was good."

Ruby and Gregory didn't spend too much more time arguing. They went back to Auckland to put the matter in the pink hands of their lawyer.

It was two days later that the next holidaymakers arrived, this time at 13 Tiritiroa. After a long discussion out on the front lawn, Mai and Poto with their Doberman and a contingent of neighbours felt a little sorry for their visitors in their singlets, baggies and jandals, and invited them in.

"You can still have your holiday, why not?" said Mai. "There's the little flat at the back and we could let you have the dinghy. It's no trouble."

The visitors were quick to decline the offer. They went away and came back two hours later with a policeman, who felt the heat but did the best he could, peering at the papers that Mai and Poto had produced, saying little. "Perhaps you should come along with me and lay a formal complaint," he suggested to the holidayers. Mai, Poto and a few of the neighbours went fishing after they'd gone.

From then on the holidaymakers kept arriving and everyone had to be alert, moving themselves from one front lawn to the next, sometimes having to break into groups so that their eyeballing skills, their skills in creative comment, could be shared around.

It was Christmas by the time the news of what was happening reached the media. The obscure local paper did a tame, muddled article on it, which was eclipsed firstly by a full page on what the mayor and councillors of the nearby town wanted for Christmas, and then by another, derived from one of the national papers, revealing New Year resolutions of fifty television personalities. After that there was the usual nationwide closedown of everything for over a month, at the end of which time no one wanted to report holiday items anymore.

So it wasn't until the new residents began to be sued that there was any news. Even then the story only trickled.

It gathered some impetus, however, when the businesspeople from the nearby town heard what was happening and felt concerned. Here was this new population at Claire Vista, or whatchyoum'callit now, who were *permanent residents* and who were *big spenders*, and here were these fly-by-night jerk holidaymakers trying to kick them out.

Well, ever since this new lot had arrived business had boomed. The town was flourishing. The old supermarket, now that there was beginning to be competition, had taken up larger premises, lowered its prices, extended its lines and was providing trolleys, music and coffee for customers. The car sale yards had been smartened up and the office decor had become so tasteful that the salespeople had had to clean themselves up and mind their language. McDonald's had bought what was now thought of as a prime business site, where they were planning to build the biggest McDonald's in the Southern Hemisphere. A couple of empty storerooms, as well as every place that could be uncovered to show old brick, had been converted into better-than-average eating places. The town's dowdy motel, not wanting to be outdone by the several new places of accommodation being built along the main road, had become pink and upmarket, and had a new board out front offering television, video, heated swimming pool, spa, waterbeds, room service, restaurant, conference and seminar facilities.

Home appliance retailers were extending their showrooms and increasing their advertising. Home building and real estate was on an upward surge as more businesspeople began to enter town and as those already there began to want bigger, better, more suitable residences. In place of dusty, paintless shops and shoppes, there now appeared a variety of boutiques, studios, consortiums, centres, lands and worlds. When the Clip Joint opened up across the road from Lulu's Hairdressers, Lulu had her place done out in green and white and it became Upper Kut. After that hair salons grew all over town, having names such as Head Office, Headlands, Beyond the Fringe, Hairport, Hairwaves, Hedlines, Siz's, Curl Up and Dye.

So the town was growing in size, wealth and reputation. Booming. Many of the new businesspeople were from the new Ikanui, the place of abundant fish. These newcomers had brought their upmarket Aussie ideas to eating establishments, accommodation, shops, cinema, pre-loved cars, newspaper publishing, transport, imports, exports, distribution. Good on them. The businesspeople drew up a petition supporting the new residents and their fine activities, and this petition was eventually signed by everyone within a twenty-kilometre radius. This had media impact.

But that wasn't all that was going on.

Billy had found other areas suitable for purchase and settlement, and Rena had done her research into the history of these areas so that they knew which of the Ngati Kangaru had ancestral ties to those places. There were six areas in the North Island and six in the South. "Think of what it does to the voting power," said Hiko, who was on the rise in local politics. Easy street, since all he needed was numbers.

Makere, who had lost her reluctance and become wholehearted, had taken Hiko's place in the company as liaison manager. This meant that she became the runner between Ozland and Aotearoa, conducting rallies, recruiting families, co-ordinating departures and arrivals. She enjoyed the work.

One day when Makere was filling in time in downtown Auckland before going to the airport, she noticed how much of the central city had closed up, gone to sleep.

"What it needs is people," she said to the rest of the family when she arrived home.

They were lounging, steaming themselves, showering, hairdressing, plucking eyebrows, in their enormous bathroom. She let herself down into the jacuzzi.

"Five hundred families to liven up the central city again. Signatures on papers, and then we turn those unwanted, wasteland wildernesses of warehouses and office spaces into town houses, penthouses and apartments." She lay back and closed her eyes. She could see the crowds once again seething in Queen Street, renamed Ara Makere, buying, selling, eating, drinking, talking, laughing, yelling, singing, going to shows. But not only in Queen Street. Not only in Auckland. Oh, it truly was high and holy work. This Kamupene o te Hokinga Mai was "a great and unwonted blessing". Mind-blowing. She sat up.

"And businesses. So we'll have to line up all our architects, designers, builders, plumbers, electricians, consultants, programmers," she said.

"'Soap boilers, tinkers and a maker of dolls' eyes'," said Billy.

"The ones already here as well as the ones still in Oz," Makere said. "Set them to work and use some of this damn money getting those places done up. Open up a whole lot of shops, restaurants, agencies..." She lay back again with her feet elevated. They swam in the spinning water like macabre fish.

"It's brilliant, Ma," Billy said, stripping off and walking across the floor with his toes turned up and his insteps arched — in fact, allowing only part of each heel and the ball joints of his big toes to touch the cold tile floor. With the stress of getting across the room on no more than heel and bone, his jaw, shoulders, elbows and knees became locked and he had a clench in each hand as well as in the bulge of his stomach.

"Those plumbers that you're talking about can come and run a few hot pipes under the floor here. Whoever built this place should've thought of that. But of course they were all summer people, so how would they know?" He lowered himself into the water, unlocking and letting out a slow, growling breath.

"We'll need different bits of paper for downtown business properties," said Tu from the steam bench.

"Central Auckland was originally Ngati Whatua I suppose," said Rena, who lost concentration on what she was doing for a moment and plucked out a complete eyebrow. "I'll check it through then arrange a hui with them."

"Think of it, we can influx any time of the year," said Billy. We can work on getting people into the city in our off-season. January...And it's not only Auckland, it's every city."

And as well as the business places there are so many houses in the cities empty at that time of the year too," said Makere, narrowing her eyes while Billy's eyes widened. "So we can look at those leaving to go on holiday as well as those leaving holiday places after the season is over. We can keep on influxing from Oz of course, but there are plenty of locals without good housing. We can round them all up — the solos, the UBs, pensioners, low-income earners, street kids, derros."

"Different papers again for suburban homes," said Tu.

"Candidates and more candidates, votes and more votes," said Hiko, who had come from next door wearing a towel and carrying a briefcase. "And why stop at Oz? We've got Maori communities in Utah, in London, all over the place."

"When do we go out snooping, Dad?" asked Hana and Gavin, who had been blow-waving each other's hair.

"Fact finding, fact finding," said Billy. "We might need three or four teams, I'll round up a few for training."

"I need a video camera," said Hana.

"Video for Hana," said Billy.

"Motorbike," said Gavin.

"Motorbike," said Billy.

"Motorbike," said Hana.

"Two motorbikes," said Billy.

"Bigger offices, more staff," said Tu and Rena.

"See to it," said Billy.

"Settlements within the cities," said Makere, who was still with solos, UBs, check-out operators and such. "Around churches. Churches, sitting there idle — wastelands, wildernesses of churches."

"And 'really of no value'," said Billy. "Until they become..."

"Meeting houses," Makere said. "Wharenui."

"Great. Redo the fronts, change the decor and we have all these new wharenui, one every block or so. Take over surrounding properties for kohanga, kura kaupapa, kaumatua housing, health and rehab centres, radio stations, TV channels..."

"Deeds of sale for church properties," said Tu.

"More party candidates as well," Hiko said. "We'll need everything in place before the new coalition government comes in..."

"And by then we'll have 'friends in high places'."

"Have our person at the top, our little surprise..."

"Who will be advised that 'it is better to reach a final and satisfactory conclusion than..."

"'...to reopen questions of strict right, or carry on an unprofitable controversy'."

"Then there's golf clubs," said Makere.

"I'll find out how many people per week, per acre use golf courses," said

Rena. "We'll find wasteland and wilderness there for sure."

"And find out how the land was acquired and how it can be reacquired," said Billy.

"Remember all the land given for schools? A lot of those schools have been closed now."

"Land given for the war effort and not returned."

"Find out who gave what and how it will be returned."

"Railways."

"Find out how much is owed to us from sale of railways."

"Cemeteries."

"Find out what we've saved the taxpayer by providing and maintaining our own cemeteries, burying our own dead. Make up claims."

"And there are some going concerns that need new ownership too, or rather where old ownership needs re-establishing..."

"Sport and recreation parks..."

"Lake and river retreats..."

"Mountain resorts..."

Billy hoisted himself. "Twenty or thirty teams and no time to waste." He splatted across the tiles. "Because 'if from delay you allow others to do it before you — they will succeed and you will fail'," and he let out a rattle and a shuffle of a laugh that sounded like someone sweeping up smashings of glass with a noisy broom.

"Get moving," he said.

Charlie the Dreaded

Briar Grace-Smith

Charlie Dread didn't eat meat and normally tried to constrict his nostrils when it was cooking but this time he allowed the smell of sizzling sausages and onions to waft inside. To caress his memory cells and release colourful pictures of past boil ups, hangis and roasts. Tender white pork, golden crackle and fat dripping running down his chin.

The warm roundness of a puku full with flesh.

"Anyone for a sausage?" called out Charlie in his soft faraway voice that nobody heard. This year Charlie had been put in charge of the sausage sizzle for the pre-Christmas day out. When Dale his sister who loved to organise had rung and told him the news he'd said "but you know I'm a vegetarian" and she'd replied "So?" then he'd said "okay then I'll do it."

Charlie Dread said okay to everything which was why he was always painting people's houses, fixing their toilets or babysitting their kids. He didn't like to take money from relations so instead people often paid him with meat that he couldn't eat. A side of mutton, a box of frozen chickens, a lump of silverside. Which he gave away. Sometimes they paid him in alcohol which he couldn't drink. Bottles of whiskey or gin...a couple dozen beer. All of this he saved for the pre-Christmas day out, they were just starting to crack it open now.

"Charlie, how are those sausages doin' Rasta mon?" It was Erena and she was heading this way. Killing him softly with her easy walk, her gingernut head of hair, her bare arms and her smile revealing a gap in her teeth so wide ten families could live there and there'd still be room to park their Toyotas.

"What you up to later Charlie?"

"Aarh not sure I'll um probably..."

"What?"

"Um I might go home, catch up on my reading."

"I thought I might have a quiet night too."

"Yeah?"

"Yeah. I might just mellow out with a video, my flatmates are away so I'll be, you know, at home. All by myself. Wouldn't mind a visitor though. Videos are more fun when you watch them with...friends."

"True," said Charlie.

"And?" Erena's arms started to fold up nastily.

"And...and and yeah maybe you should get a friend to come over."

"Hey Charlie. You better watch that sausage. It might burn," she hissed marching back to the crowd, grabbing a twist top on her way and opening it unnecessarily with the gap in her teeth, all the time giving him a look that he just didn't understand.

"One day," thought Charlie still reeling from the encounter, "one day I'm gonna ask that girl out."

Over by the picnic table Dale and Joe were having a domestic. They'd been together since college but the fire between them had died long ago leaving nothing but the smell of damp ashes and a relationship that had become a bad habit. They were a pair of captive animals, each holding the key to the other one's cage but refusing to set it free. They were arguing now about that fated party two months ago when Joe had walked Dale's friend Carol home.

"Come and sort this out Charlie bro you were with us that night, did I go home with Carol?" moaned Joe, rolling his eyes around in their sockets, daring Charlie to say yes.

"Tell me Charlie, did he go inside with her?" pleaded Dale stiffening her spine, sticking out her chin. Daring him to say no.

Charlie Dread looked down at his bare feet and wished there was a hole nearby he could jump into. There was no hole so he shut his eyes and pretended he was in one instead. Then something hard prodded and poked at him digging beneath his ribcage and forcing his eyes open. "Aarh!"

Charlie always got a fright when he saw his father these days, since his kidneys cut out last year, his skin had turned a strange grey black. He looked like someone who'd been pulled out of the deep freeze. A living dead person who could smile and walk. There he was off balance wheezing like Darth Vader, waving and stabbing his tokotoko around in the air like a laser sword.

"Aarh!" screamed Charlie again fending off the tokotoko.

"You all right son?"

"Yeah Dad, it's a bit hot over this grill that's all."

"While you're there, how about a couple of those sausages eh? Lots of sauce and some of that white bread and don't forget, plenty butter."

"Um...that stuff's not good for you Dad..."

"Shut up and give me the damn sausage, I'm gonna die anyway."

"Well then how about some of this juice to wash it down with?"

"What sort of juice?"

"It's aarh Ital Vital juice Dad"

"What the hell is that?" asked Dad flaring his nostrils in premeditated disgust.

"Celery and beetroot, just the stuff to purify the blood and clean out kidneys."

"Bugger off," said his dad putting some bread on his butter, squirting on half the bottle of tomato sauce for flavour then adding a shake or five of salt and biting into his magnificent creation with huge satisfaction.

"Just what the doctor ordered," he choked between bites.

"Jah," Charlie asked his god, "how can I help change the world when I can't even make my old man drink a glass of juice, when I haven't the courage to tell my sister the truth?"

With that he cleaned up the barbecue, stacked the cooked sausages tidily on their plate, tucked his bible under his arm and found a spot in the park where he could relax, read and find divine inspiration.

There was a place that Charlie Dread fell into while reading the holy book that day. As the people around him swam, sang and ate cold sausages the letters on the pages turned into curious shapes and the rustle of the flax and the song of cicadas hungry for love saturated him with their music. The island that sat darkly between him and the horizon turned jungle green and became so clear that Charlie could see every ponga tree, every pohutukawa bleeding red with flower. He could even see the ranger's four wheel drive climbing up a dirt track like a blue ant.

"Someone must've laced my beetroot juice," Charlie's thoughts said loudly. Then "nah, they know I'm not into hard drugs."

A rasta coloured tunnel sprang from a cloud suspended above the sea and he was blinded by its glare.

A feather brushed lightly across his lips making them wet and hungry.

Someone was there.

Standing over him speckled wings raised, wearing a crown of thorns and woven dreadlocks, stood an angel. His skin was the colour of Desert Road earth. All shades of brown rolled into one. A sarong of red, gold and green covered him waist down.

"Charlie," the flax around him whispered.

"Charlie," the cicadas sang.

"I am Reikorangi. The lion lives inside you. Call him out," they chorused together.

The angel put his head close to Charlie's holding him still with his eyes, like a lion's, gentle and strong, but with a lick of danger floating in their amber depths.

"I love you but don't piss me off" kind of eyes.

And slowly the angel retreated into the coloured tunnel of light, vacuumed neatly back up, into the candy floss cloud he came from.

And as if someone had snatched a pair of magic 3-D glasses from his eyes the normality of Charlie's world returned.

The island became faraway and small once more and the voices of cicada and flax turned back into music and sound. Only Charlie was left altered feeling somehow energised and awake. A vision he thought. He'd had a vision.

"Yes. Fuck yes. We'll have a game of rugby then," Joe was bellowing, "and once you get dicked maybe you'll shut up...hey we could use Erena's teeth as the goal post. First one through the gap." Joe was on a roll now, violating Charlie's after-vision euphoria with swearing and disrespectful imagery.

"Get real." It was Erena. It was Erena. It was Erena.

"We'll waste you pack of losers and we'll have Charlie on our side, thank you."

What? Here he was, Charlie Dread, feeling as wobbly as a newborn foal and she wanted him to play rugby? Maybe he was still dreaming, trapped between vision and reality. But he wasn't because suddenly she was standing over him.

A million freckles dancing under her red hair.

"Chaaarlie," she said slow and sweet.

"We, the women, have just had a bet with the…men that we can beat them in a game of rugby. First to score."

"What?"

"Dale and Joe had this big fight, well you know how she used to play for the Black Ferns and went to England? She reckons that Joe's always been jealous of her which is why he went off with Carol that night."

"This is crazy," sighed Charlie.

"Well just what happens when someone as horny as Joe walks someone as horny as Carol home then? They go inside drink Horlicks and play Monopoly all night? I don't think so. But what am I telling you for? You know what happened, you were there."

Charlie held his head between his hands and squeezed hard, trying to pop out the pictures of Joe and Carol, but they stayed inside like stubborn pus. There they were, walking in front of him. There was Joe his arm wrapped tightly around Carol's waist whistling the tune to "Mustang Sally" and Carol laughing and leaning into Joe's shoulder, touching his hair, running her fingers under his collar and there was Joe again giving Charlie the signal to get lost from behind his back. Then Charlie watching from the letterbox as they walked inside. Together.

"You know Charlie," said Erena. "It doesn't matter how bad a relationship is, you shouldn't cheat."

"I know."

"Then stop sitting on fences."

"He's my friend."

"He used you. He hurt your sister. I'm pretty sure it's not the first time."

"What's a game of rugby gonna do?"

"Release some steam, stop them from killing each other when they get home. Get up we need you Charlie."

"I haven't played in years."

"I need you then Charlie. Did you hear me? I NEED YOU. So get outta that flax bush and do something about it!"

Joe and the other men took off their shirts. That way it'd be easier to tell the teams apart they reckoned.

"Yeah right," laughed Erena. "You just wanna show off your beer pots."

Joe retaliated by laughing and cracking jokes about Charlie playing for the women. He was trying to act relaxed and cool but his voice was weak and his face shone with sweat. Everybody knew he was shitting himself.

Dale looked like she was gonna take on the entire opposition by herself. Crouched down haka style with her lavalava tucked into her shorts she had one eye on the ball, another on the opposition and the one in the back of her head was planted firmly on her own team. She was the only experienced player they had.

"Spread out," she screamed.

"What does that mean dear?" It was Peg Leg Polly playing halfback.

Charlie tied back his dreadlocks nervously. Things looked bad, him, Dale and Erena were the only ones on their side not physically challenged and under fifty years old. Dale would be counting on him, what if he messed up?

Kickoff came and went like thunder. Joe's team had the ball. It went from Joe to Macky to Wiremu to big Uncle Rua and Erena! Erena was on Uncle Rua and he was shaking her off like dandruff and and...and...oh no she was down hitting the ground with a thump and he was through...Big Uncle Rua was through and going for the try line.

"On him Charlie! On him!" shrieked Dale. "But what about Peg Leg Polly, she's here too," thought Charlie. "Why don't you yell at her? She's just standing there...on one foot."

"Charlie, Charlie, call on the lion," hummed the cicadas, breathed the flax.

"On him, on him you chickenshit!" screeched Dale.

"The lion, call on the lion," whispered the flax sung the cicadas.

Help, thought Charlie help help help and, stuff this, as Uncle Rua crashed forward, ten tons of sinew and untamed muscle.

"The lion," the flax and cicadas harmonised, "bring on the lion."

"Lion," begged Charlie, looking towards the sky, "please come out, come out" and then, leaping forward like bungy elastic, Charlie Dread was on Uncle Rua. A brick wall. Knocking him to the ground. Leaving him black eyed, bloody lipped and swimming in stars and now the ball...the ball!

The ball was out rolling from Uncle Rua's large flat hands like a runaway orange and Macky was about to scoop but no! She was first! Dale had the ball and she was outta there, smoking up the field behind her yelling "back me up back me up!"

The opposition stood open jawed and unprepared, a pack of stunned kereru while Dale, a wily tirairaka, dodged and darted between them. Only Joe was ready for her. He'd been expecting something like this. He waited for her as she approached the try line. He waited for her and moved in for the hit. Dale could see in his eyes he was gonna make this tackle a hard one and she could see in his eyes he was guilty. "Pig," she spat. "Two-timing pig."

"So what," he said silently. "She wants me, you don't. You can't even look at me anymore," and with his head down and aimed at her stomach he charged like a bull.

And why not? Nothing mattered now win or lose they were over and it sucked. But did she care? Did Dale even care? If she did she never let on and he needed to see her hurt.

Dale hardened her abs against the impact and curled her body into itself like a hedgehog but she never stopped thinking not for a second, and just before she went down she passed the ball out, straight and strong praying "please be there Charlie, please be there."

How Charlie Dread made it up the field fast enough to catch that pass is a mystery but he did and feeling the ball light and smooth in his hands he sprinted towards the try line. And although there was nobody who could touch his shadow or even catch the tail end of his breeze he didn't slow down. Charlie Dread flew over that line with all the skill, grace and force of a lion. They'd won!

But the funny thing was that when the game was over nobody clapped, cheered or teased. The brilliance of the play didn't matter. Neither did the miracle of Charlie's try.

It was hard to celebrate victory when it walked hand in hand with bruised egos and broken hearts. Dale and Joe were both in pain and the friendship they'd all shared had changed when the group had taken sides. Nothing would be the same.

Charlie cleaned up the barbecue and packed it into his father's ute.

In the thick hot afternoon dampness the sound of Erena's voice was a sword cutting into cream cake. "You did good Charlie Dread."

"Thanks."

"I always suspected you were a dark horse."

Charlie shrugged.

"I mean it," Erena teased. "You're not the same guy I spoke to this morning."

Embarrassed but proud Charlie rolled his dozing father onto his back, helped him to his feet and pushed him, wheezing, into the passenger seat. Grabbing the keys and jumping inside, he rolled the window down, looked Erena straight in the eye with all the confidence of Muhammad Ali and said "Hey Erena, you still watching videos tonight?"

"Yeah...why?" Erena poked her tongue through her gap and for once turned as red as her hair.

"Well I was gonna say aarh..."

"What Charlie?"

"I aaarh...um I..." Where was that frigging lion when Charlie needed it most?

"Speak Charlie, speak!" Erena's red and bashful cheeks were changing their shade, turning darker and more dangerous. The colour of full blown frustration.

"I hope you have a good time that's all," blurted Charlie, freaking out, sliding the ute into gear and speeding off.

"One day," thought Charlie Dread looking at the love of his life through the rear view mirror stomping dirt and giving him the fingers.

"One day I'm gonna ask that girl out."

Life As It Really Is

Witi Ihimaera

It will help if you are White, blue-eyed, blond and cute with a nice butt. If you're a woman, you will need to be, similarly, White, blue-eyed, blonde, what is known as a "babe" and under twenty-five. Because the camera photographs you heavier than you actually are, girls will need to be as anorexic as possible. The more you look like Barbie the better. Don't worry about any physical imperfections as these can be fixed. Be prepared to have your teeth straightened, nose bobbed, jaw wired, boobs siliconed, waist scalpeled and any individuality you might have possessed plastic-surgeoned out altogether. The object is not to look different but to look the same as the other boys and dolls who inhabit the world.

Should you not fit the physical criteria above *viz* you are bald, fat and plain, don't worry. You still have a part to play. However, it will not be as the main actor or actress in life's drama. This does not necessarily mean that you cannot make it. Barbara Streisand, surely one of the world's most oddest looking women — but she could sing. The fantasy of the ugly duckling who becomes a swan is for most of us a drama that is ironically only purveyed by a society obsessed, in fact, with beauty. Once an ugly duckling, always an ugly duckling. So best to resign yourself to being the Friend of the Star, or the Comic Relief or the Mother of the Star.

If you are a person of colour, you need not apply unless you're tall, black and stupid enough to think you matter. Otherwise, forget it. Remember your pride and let those White folks go ahead and pick a White actor to play the villain.

You may have to sleep with the director or the producer or the associate producer or the casting director, no matter how foul-breathed or cocaine-smashed he (or she) might be. Don't bother with the scriptwriter as he has no power as far as casting is concerned. If you're a young girl, try to remember that it's all over in five minutes and, after all, what's five minutes if you are guaranteed stardom? If you're a boy, grit your teeth and just remember that some of life's great stars played their first starring roles with their jeans around their ankles. Whoever you are, four pieces of advice: try not to chew gum, do not under any circumstances make any reference to his toupee, make him believe his is the biggest you've ever seen and don't forget to have the bastard sign your contract before you let him in.

If you are a person of colour, the above route also applies if you are really desperate to get that job as a maid, Mexican bandit, the girl who gets shot so that the White hero can go back to marry the White woman in the last reel.

Should you have been stupid enough to be saddled with your childhood sweetheart, or married him (or her) or have had a teenage pregnancy, don't worry. That's what your publicity agent is for. Your agent will evaluate all the dumb things you did before you got into the business and either fix it (i.e., love doesn't go with the business, so out goes the teenage sweetheart) or put a positive spin on it (i.e., your teenage spouse couldn't take your new career so you both agreed that, for his sake and yours, you both have to part). Having been pregnant is okay, as long as it was illegitimate. This helps give you a reputation. However, under no circumstances will you be allowed to be photographed with your child as this will only detract from your image and reveal that you are older than you look.

None of the above applies if you are a person of colour.

When you report for work, do not expect a set which at all resembles reality. Life is a movie, for God's sake, didn't your Momma tell you? But don't worry. At every script meeting before you are shot (on film and by the camera, that is) your friendly coke supplier will be on hand to give you a fix that will get you through the day.

When you walk onto the set the lights that are blazing don't come from the sun. Get used to the light as it is the only kind you'll see for the rest of your life. Everything around you will be artificial. The mountains, rivers, houses are all fake and most of the time they're only frontages. None of the doorways or roads lead to anywhere. There's nothing behind the facades you work in.

The costumes you wear will have been worn by others who have appeared in similar life stories. Sometimes, when you put them on you can catch a whiff of the scent of the person who has worn the costume before you. None of the jewellery is real.

Sometimes your script might lead you to believe you will be going to Italy or filming in Tibet. Most times, however, all the filming will take place on the backlot of Hollywood USA. Don't look too closely at anything around you. It will not be what you think it is but, rather, a phantom construct, something without any substance.

At other times you will find yourself acting in front of a blue screen delivering dialogue in a setting that isn't really there to people who are not able to be on the set on the day. They do incredible things with computer-isated special effects these days. The most amazing simulacrums have been developed and you will be surprised, when you see the rushes, to see yourself delivering your dialogue to Madonna or Cher or any other ghosts who are appearing in your film. Nothing is real. Nobody is real. Madonna and Cher don't, in fact, exist.

Do not expect any intelligence in the script. Above all, do not question the script or the way the director wants you to deliver your lines. The director is God and he knows better than you do how you should portray your life. His idea of great dialogue is for you to say "Wow!" or "Great!" or "Oh, wow!" for maximum emotional effect. Be prepared to spout the most inane, stupid, incredibly unbelievable load of shit you've ever read.

If you are a person of colour you are lucky. You are not given lines as such but, rather, your part will consist of reaction shots, grunts and body poses. Thus, if you are dumb, no problem.

You will not need to know how to act. There are basically only four facial expressions to master. The first is the "I love you" expression. For this you widen your eyes, let your lips go slack, run your fingers through your hair and look yearningly at the camera. The second is the "I hate you" expression. In this one you widen your eyes even wider, let your lips go slack, run your fingers through your hair (you must have *lots* of hair if you want to be successful in life) and look yearningly at the camera so that everybody knows you want to escape the jerk playing opposite you. The third expression is the "I'm in danger" expression. This is the same expression as the "I love you" expression.

The fourth expression is the "Now we can go home" expression, which you save for the end of the picture. In this one you really have the opportunity to emote. The best way to obtain this expression is to think of yourself as Lassie waiting to be given a bone. You widen your eyes, let your lips go slack, run your fingers through your hair — if you have any left — and look yearningly at the camera. Why they ever need humans I'll never know. Computer images do the job just as well these days.

Have you thought of other positions in the industry? For those prepared to kill themselves there's always stunt work. For those interested in design, all stars need somebody to make them look good. If you are the kind of musician who doesn't mind composing with novocaine, this industry is made for you.

Be prepared for nude scenes. For those with a perfect set of boobs or the perfect (White) penis but with unfortunate looks in every other department, you will be able to find work as a body part.

If you are a person of colour take note that while equality was achieved years ago very few directors will allow you to actually be seen in bed with a White partner.

You have three choices of scenario. The first is the romantic drama which may be in costume or contemporary dress or, if X-rated, no costume or dress at all. The main actors will get the best lines and the best costumes. The rest of you will be colour coded according to the designer's idea of what will best accessorise the main actors. Nobody needs to worry about acting. All the men need to do is to strike heroic poses. The women need only to heave their bosoms and scream while waiting for the hero to rescue you. If you are appearing in an X-rated movie, you have no lines at all. If you are a person of colour you die.

The second is the action drama, which may be period, Western, thriller, horror or kung-fu. The action drama is a lot of fun. Again you don't need to know about acting. The gadgets and special effects take this role over. All the men need to do is to know how to jump through windows, escape blazing aeroplanes, stop the bomb from going off and fight the villain. The women need only to heave their bosoms, scream for help and, in the horror movie, it's pretty inevitable that you will be the victim in the gory slash sequences. There's nothing better than to see a young girl being cut up by the killer. If you are a person of colour — and if you're not Will Smith — you are the villain and you die.

The third is the fantasy drama, including animation (the new word for cartoons) or space opera. In this one, the main actor must look like Harrison Ford or a handsome(r) American president than Clinton because, as we all know, all space operas are really about America saving the planet from an evil intergalactic force. Be prepared to make lofty statements, delivered deadpan and to soaring music as you face almost insurmountable odds. The women need only to heave their bosoms if they are playing the wicked part or act the virgin if they are playing the princess part. Interestingly, the person of colour, like Hiawatha or Jafar or Moses, has actually become a hero, but only if he or she appears in a cartoon. Failing that, her or she is cast to type — as an animal like the Lion King or, as what happened to Whoopi Goldberg, a hyena. However, in a live action drama we're back to basics. This type of drama is best avoided if you want to live a long life. They are usually written to a very bad formula in which you have a few words of dialogue and then a chase scene which ends with an explosion. After this come another few words of dialogue and chase scene and greater explosion. Third time around, there are more words of dialogue, another chase and an even greater explosion than before. An incredible number of cars are disposed of in such movies. So are a *lot* of people who just happen to be flying on the plane that gets hijacked or the train that goes off the rails or the ship that sinks. Still, it's fun for the spectators.

If you are a person of colour you are the sidekick in the detective thriller, the second lead in the space opera, you don't get the princess, you live long enough to congratulate the hero for saving the world and then you die.

If you are lucky enough your first picture will be a hit. Should this occur you must let your publicity agent run your career. He (or she) will tell you what to do, where to go and what kind of image you are supposed to present to an adoring public. The problem will be that this image will stay with you for life. Only a few manage to escape the typecasting but not everyone is a Meryl Streep or Dustin Hoffmann. The rest will remain trapped either as eternal blonde-headed virgin — or worse, Farrah Fawcett, still a bimbo at fifty and with all that hair — or as the eternal golden boy like Robert Redford (Brad Pitt, beware).

You will be asked to pose for front covers where every blemish of face and body has been digitally removed and you become somebody you do not recognise saying things you never recognise as coming out of your sweet little mouth. This is when you can start reading about yourself, the fun you're having with people you've never met and the affairs you've started with people you don't know. If at all possible avoid believing in the stories about yourself. Do what the others do — begin wearing dark glasses and try to avoid photographers and your public. Otherwise they will ask questions about a life you are not leading which you won't be able to answer. Not only that, but do you really want to be associated with the crap you are supposed to have said?

By this stage, you may well be advised to get married — preferably to your leading man (or woman) or to the director. This is called life imitating the movie and your public will love the idea that two people who met while filming, say, *Titanic* may have been drowned on the screen but found true lurve while doing it.

Marrying your director is second best — but okay. Such marriages only confirm, anyway, that you got the part not because of any talent you have but because the director fell in lust with your picture in a magazine or wanted to play Svengali with you. The golden rule is to accept a director's proposal. If you don't, he can spread the word around that you are difficult and, honey, if that happens you won't get another job in this town. After a few years you can ditch the bastard anyway with a quickie divorce in Las Vegas and do him for as much alimony as you can get.

Marriage will also help your career at this stage because it will prove that you are not gay or lesbian and, rather, a regular guy or gal. While life says it's okay to be sexually ambivalent best not to Come Out. Nobody wants to see a faggot kissing a sex goddess like Pamela Anderson on the screen. It's not Pammie's fault when the audience starts to snicker. They all know that the guy who's kissing her would rather be kissing the hunky gardener.

Persons of colour don't need a publicity agent. Everybody knows they are dumb. Nor will they appear on a front cover unless it's *Ebony* magazine. Kissing Pamela Anderson? Get real.

If you should still have aspirations to be the main actor in any of the above but have been relegated to the sidelines, never fear. Television may be just the right place for you, especially as a news presenter where, because you are always photographed front on, you need no torso or profile. If there's no room in TV-land, tough. Life wasn't meant to be easy.

Five years later you will be thirty and in mid-career. If you're lucky you will still be on the big screen. If not, you'll be on a series like "The Young and the Brainless" or, by now, have faded into the back row of the extras or else become the adoring public at premieres at the Mann Chinese Theatre.

You will now be onto your second marriage (there are another two or three to go) and your body, while still okay, may be looking the worse for wear and tear. Little things may need to be fixed or adjusted, so if you are still a star, be prepared for a mid-career nip and tuck. Some men that I know have their lives so tied up with their ego that they go further and have penile implants or extensions. The problem is that plastic surgery, however, goes only so far. Surgeons can fix the face but from the neck down the prognosis isn't good. However, full body transplants are just around the corner and, very soon, you'll be able to get your head attached to some fresh new body recently harvested out of Eastern Europe. When the technology is available have no remorse about receiving your new body. You'll probably make better use of it than its previous owner anyway.

Be prepared for your first visit (wearing dark glasses so that the news photographers won't know it's you) to the Betty Ford Clinic for drug or alcohol addiction. Don't let this get you down. After all, better people than you have trodden the same path — and Elizabeth Taylor met a garage mechanic at Betty's.

To help your flagging career, widen your interests so that people realise that you have the world's future at heart. Support a charity. AIDS work has already gone and so has raising money to save the starving children of Africa. Make sure that whatever you choose is empathetic. Something like "Save the Rabbits of the World" will do just fine.

By the time you're forty you will have become a veteran in your world. You will start playing older parts. You will also be watching younger men and women of little talent taking your place. Although you might want to poison their drinks at the next cocktail party try to desist. They will get everything they deserve.

Some very few actually manage to survive life with some distinction. Listen to the tale of ravishing red-headed actress Rhonda Fleming. She played the typical American dream. She was born in Hollywood, made some good films and bad films, married four times and in her last marriage achieved apotheosis — as the wife of Ten Mann, owner of the Mann Chinese Theatre on Sunset Boulevard.

Not everybody can marry a movie house owner, however. For most of you, remember that after you turn fifty (I'm being charitable here) you are not supposed to exist. The best idea, therefore, is to kill yourself in a car accident like James Dean or take sleeping pills like Marilyn Monroe. It worked for them. After all, they are better known in death than they were in life.

But if you're a coward and still around, clear the set willya?

And if you're a person of colour don't worry.

Nobody notices the cleaner.

Wairua is designed to flow in a Koru style

Zion A. Komene

Weaving letters into words was a skill which came easily to Matua Jobey. So when he faced off against himself on the Scrabble board, just before the phone rang to say his only son Taniora was dead, he knew he didn't need to refer to the dictionary for metaphors.

It wasn't that he didn't feel a twinge inside. A deep paternal bond calling to let him know his son of twenty-two years was gone. "Aue," exclaimed Matua Jobey as he laid the Scrabble pieces on the board. He shifted the creamy coloured squares of plastic letters back and forth to spell ANECDOTAL.

"That's a nine-letter spin for me. Aueee, I'm too much sometimes!" smiled Matua Jobey.

No. There was nothing super duper special about Matua Jobey knowing Taniora had died. Sure, the sky went grey and thunder clapped overhead. And the ruru were in the trees all day, hooting like crazy. But the owls always delivered messages to Matua Jobey. Even during the day.

Nope. Nothing surprised Matua Jobey. He could sense when the earth moved before the earth moved. That's why he was always prepared for earthquakes that never occurred.

Matua Jobey existed in a state of perpetual balance on his own personal Richter scale. He was the mercury in the thermometer that always stayed cool.

So when Karli slobbered over the phone that Taniora had been bowled by a drunk driver while on his early evening jog along Remuera Settlement Road, Matua Jobey didn't lose it.

He did what he always did. He got methodical. And dealt with it. Matua Jobey collected all the Scrabble pieces. With infinite care he placed them in the box. Like a Priest turning the pages of a Bible, or a Kaumatua preparing to whaikorero over the body of a loved one. He gently folded the Scrabble board in half, let it slide into the Scrabble box. He sealed the box with the lid. Then he put on his shoes and coat and walked out the door, gently but firmly closing it behind him.

Matua Jobey wasn't always methodical. There were times when he called it how he saw it. Especially when he had his own five-piece jazz band. They called themselves the Manuka Quintet. Don't ask me why they named their band after this particular native tree. I mean, they had the pick of tall, proud, defiant trees like kauri or totara. Not a twisted piece of firewood.

Maybe they thought of themselves as "young, virile strong saplings trying to break through the canopy of conventional jazz rainforest". Well at least that was the question the reporter from the local newspaper put to the Manuka Quintet back in February 1958. The question seemed inspired. But Tane "Four Fingers and One Thumb" Taylor, who wanted to play the piano in the band but for obvious reasons had to settle for the bass, attempted to answer it. As a result, any real meaning got lost somewhere between the large gulf separating Uncle Tane's explanation and the reporter's comprehension.

"Well see, I was an axeman eh?" grunted Uncle Tane, swinging his heavy bass on a ninety-degree angle, adjusting his eyebrows as he measured the reporter. "Used to chop manuka for firewood. Nah. We don't say we're the Manuka Quintet cos we wanna remember what it's like to be wet and cold in the bush. Who wants to remember that? Eh, can't you speak English? It's can of peas."

According to Matua Jobey, Uncle Tane was a pretty icy kinda person back then.

Age hasn't thawed him either.

"Is that how you lost the thumb?" asked the reporter tentatively. "Nah," said Uncle Tane, "I lost it at the freezing works when I was a butcher. Dunno where it went. Probably ended up in a sausage on someone's table."

After that story appeared in the headlines it was pretty much self-explanatory what happened. The fledgling musical career envisaged by the Manuka Quintet remained just that. Fledgling. They played the occasional Buffalo Lodge social and local Marae socials. Sometimes family twenty-firsts and weddings. For a while there wherever the Manuka Quintet played they were showered with sausages by the audience. That was back when two shillings could buy a dozen of Porangi Thomas' snarler sausages. These days Porangi Thomas' snarlers are an institution. A designer accessory for the young and well educated who want to tap into their British consciousness at Sunday brunch. Totally unaware that Porangi Thomas is half-Irish. And befitting their Establishment status, it now costs around five bucks for five "Snarler Classics". A lot of old timers Matua Jobey's age usually want to throw something else at Porangi Thomas' butcher shop in protest at the inflated price.

The Manuka Quintet didn't last much longer after that. Not that it worried Matua Jobey. He considered he had a relationship of greater substance with his saxophone. So after the Manuka Quintet broke up and each went his separate way, Uncle Jobey retreated to his house, out the back of Waiwera Road. He closed all the doors and poured a cup of strong black tea from the pot. (Even though it was only tea, the way Matua Jobey made it you would have thought it was homemade whisky. It always made me involuntarily stand to attention every time I took a gulp.)

Of course all this is just hearsay. I mean I wasn't there. For all I know Matua Jobey jumped all over his saxophone, threw it away and substituted the tea for Johnny Walker Black Label. And proceeded to stay drunk for twelve years until I was born.

But knowing Matua Jobey real well, I imagine him back in 1958, after the last dregs of tea are tossed out the window into the garden. Matua Jobey shakes himself loose and sits slightly forward. He rubs his saxophone with his shirt sleeve until he can see his hands in the shiny silver. Matua Jobey sits in the window, releasing lyrical notes into the warm summer night. Saxophone soul wafts through the walls, up the chimney and through the windows. The breeze billows Matua Jobey's cadence of thought up to Putahi Mountain. To call to our ancestors lying in the cave. Not to tell them to get up or anything mind you. More just to say, things are okay. Your children live well. No one forgets.

My mind's eye captures Matua Jobey after the last note is played in 1958. To fastforward back to the future. To 1998. Where the land lies in the darkness of Now Time. And whispers of old saxophone jazz reverberate over the topography of Putahi Mountain.

Matua Jobey takes off his shirt and trousers, folds them neatly onto the

163

bedroom chair, sets the alarm clock to fall off the bedside drawer at 5.30 a.m. He softly rubs the tips of his fingers over the picture of Auntie Raina, lets the static electricity generate through his fingertips into his being. Chuckling at the memories he captures, Matua Jobey piles himself into bed and allows sleep to come easily.

But the reality of Matua Jobey, of what made him who he was, cut across my imagination with all the surgical sharpness and precision of an AFFCO boning knife. Especially when he knocked on my door at 8.15 p.m. Thursday evening to tell me Taniora was dead.

"I read the signs Boy. But I wasn't listening. I should've been with him." Matua Jobey was a stickler for keeping appointments. Especially ones concerning life and death.

"You're always there for everyone Matua," I said as I laced up my boots and buttoned my coat. "Whenever something's happening you're the Man." I hugged my Uncle long and deep. It's never been easy for me to accept the touch of another. But I am always happy to greet Matua Jobey, either with hongi or strong hugs. It's never mattered. Because it's true, you know. Whenever we have needed help, Matua Jobey has always been there.

Of course the level of help needed by us sometimes didn't equate with the level required. Maybe people just felt comforted in the knowledge that our Matua was there supporting us. Perhaps everyone viewed Matua Jobey as a kind of link to our past. Like an electronic card key, where if you slid it along the access box just so, the door would open. And you received entry for a moment, into a world long gone.

Whatever the case, whenever the load of life needed to be lightened a little, it all seemed much easier if you talked it over with Matua Jobey first. For instance when the Teina brothers decided their work crew was going to clean our sacred river they knew they had to do the right thing.

So one Thursday morning at 5:00 a.m. before the sun rose, Matua Jobey and the work crew all gathered on the grass banks of the Waitangi River, below the Marae. As the last breath of night wind softly blew away the morning stars hanging low in the horizon, Matua Jobey intoned the karakia to bless the work crew and their endeavours to cleanse our spiritual waters.

I can't remember everything Matua Jobey said, but somewhere during the long incantation, to Ihoa O Nga Mano, the Creator of all things, to all of our ancestors, to the living, and to those yet to come, the sound of the river warbling past us seemed to resonate with a clear, almost Sony CD audio quality. It was as if the river was saying, Gee thanks for cleaning me. After a hundred and fifty years. What's the catch?

Maybe that's why all the problems occurred after the karakia. All the work crew started dropping like flies. Huge boils popped up all over the bodies of the young men digging and tearing up the trees and shrubs colonising our river. The Teina brothers shrugged it off. Until Rawiri Teina stumbled out of his housebus one morning screaming and holding the left side of his butt. Jutting out of his Moerewa Tigers rugby league shorts was a searing red boil the size of a tennis ball.

"It's the river. Must be angry at us or sumthin," muttered Rawiri as he stood and manoeuvred the rear view mirror on his car to inspect the boil on his butt. This hypothesis was confirmed in Rawiri's mind when his brother Redd kicked out the door to his housebus, rubbing the right side of his butt, screaming and cursing like a banshee.

"Gee I really feel for you boys," chuckled Matua Jobey when he heard about the work crew. "Lessee," he said, going through an inventory of everything that had occurred before the epidemic of boiled butts had hit home. "Did you come across anything in the river? Any of you fish up any bones or find some old taonga?" Matua Jobey scratched his head and pondered, "Hmmm, never heard of a plague of boils here in Aotearoa before. Only in Egypt. No one here named Moses?" And he looked around suspiciously.

Redd Teina tightened his belt buckle to his jeans. "Has someone put a makutu on us Uncle?" The work crew all looked at Redd then at Matua Jobey. Dezay knotted the sleeves to his black woollen jersey he had tied around his head. Jimmy stuffed the legs of his jeans into his thick woollen socks then secured them with his big heavy workboots. All the boys wore the same kind of heavy denim uniform that stayed on their bodies until it fell off. Like Gregorian monks they were dedicated to black attire and wore it religiously during work and after hours. Unlike any kind of order dedicated to piety, the boys took great pleasure to adorn their bodies with tattoos of snakes draped around etchings vaguely resembling the human female form. While their black T-shirts were adorned with iron-on decals of skulls and phrases like BAD TO THE BONE, all courtesy of Big Oggie's Tee Print shop.

"If it's a curse Boy then it's easily remedied," replied Matua Jobey to an anxious Redd Teina. "Tell us what we need to do Matua," said Rawiri Teina, clenching the remaining eleven teeth in his mouth, bracing himself for the herculean feats he was sure he would need to perform. Rawiri was the kind of guy who, if he could, would have scaled our sacred mountain. Forged through our sacred river. Walked our sacred land from one end to the other. But you never saw him wash the dishes or change nappies.

Matua Jobey sighed. "First things first boys. You will need to bathe in our river. Let the water be your friend." The work crew looked at one another, shrugged, closed their eyes and amongst a verbal shower of "ooh ahh it's friggin cold," they tiptoed into the river.

"Ahh, but you have to get all of those clothes off too eh? The water has to touch every part of you eh?" said Matua Jobey, his voice ringing in the crisp morning air. "Let our river talk to you boys. Get kanohi ki te kanohi!! Eye to eye boys!! Eye to eye!!"

With his bald head and tall heavy frame Matua Jobey could have been Gautama Buddha standing at the banks of the River Ganges contemplating a Nirvana existence.

Instead he was Matua Jobey trying to teach the twentysomething-year-old children of his nieces and nephews the benefits of using soap.

"Now take this boys," said Matua Jobey as he ripped apart a couple of six packs of Palmolive Gold soap bars he had booked up on Karli's account at Molly Strakhan's Four Square store. Like one of the disciples tossing bread and fish to the multitudes, Matua Jobey hurled the soap bars to the work crew.

"Wash all that makutu off you. That's the bugger!!" Matua Jobey proclaimed as he stalked the banks of the river, looking more like Julius Caesar haughtily surveying the Celtic hordes across a Gaul river tributary, than a man of seventy-two trying to teach his backwater grandnephews how to wash properly.

After making sure they all took turns scrubbing one another's backs, Matua Jobey summoned the work crew out of the water. They straggled out, pale and shivering, the water a creamy milky colour from the soap. The shock of the cold sharpened their senses, making them acutely aware of their surroundings. Karli and Auntie Kataraina wrapped each one in a towel and handed out cups of hot steaming kawakawa tea to clean themselves from within.

But Matua Jobey pulled Rawiri Teina aside. Instead of wrapping him in a towel he folded Rawiri in a korowai feather cloak. Weaved from flax and adorned with dark black feathers tipped with curls of white, the cloak radiated agelessness. It was so big it could have fit two Rawiris in it. And Rawiri was over six foot tall. Matua Jobey secured the cloak around Rawiri's neck, placed his hands on Rawiri's shoulders. The two men pressed foreheads and noses in hongi, and Matua Jobey stepped back from a pleasantly startled Rawiri.

"He kakahu tenei o to whanau, Boy," smiled Matua Jobey to Rawiri. "Your great-grandfather pulled me from this river, right here when I was eight years old. I was drowning. I almost died. He slapped his huge hands on my back to make me cough up our river. Your great-grandfather said to me, 'Next time pull the mana of the river into you. Not its lifeblood. You'll only choke on it.' Then he wrapped me in this cloak. It has warmed me for the last sixty-four years Boy. Now it'll warm you." And Matua Jobey and Rawiri settled down on the banks of our river to talk of mana and makutu and the life designs people weave, while the work crew warmed themselves with the tea, in the late morning sun.

Later that day after the makutu was put to rest, and Karli and Auntie Kataraina had doused the old forlorn denim rags in kerosene and Bic flicked them, the work crew dressed in freshly ironed blue denim jeans and black leather jackets and accompanied Matua Jobey to the Waitangi Pub.

Matua Jobey wandered into the Garden Bar and pulled up a chair next to me. He placed the Scrabble game on the table. "Hey hey hey," I said. "Kia ora ra Matua. How's things? You deal to those troubled voices in our river?" I poured the Scrabble pieces onto the table, making sure none landed in my beer handle of raspberry and lemonade. I turned the creamy plastic letters face down on the table.

Matua Jobey nodded my way, slowly placing his hands on the Scrabble board, rubbing his fingertips on its shiny surface. "I dealt to them all right eh Boy. But I don't know. We left a lot of soap in the river eh? Can't be doing its circulatory system any good." Matua Jobey twirled a couple of Scrabble pieces in his fingers. "Hey how do you spell circulatory anyway Boy?"

On certain occasions if Matua Jobey felt that ceremony was uncalled for, he would cut to the chase, sweep away all the detritus of social norms, action and acceptance, to reveal the truth of the matter. In compact form. Plain and simple. For all to see.

Like the time when Riana, who was known as Tariana back in '91, who was known as Maia back in '87, who started out life to those who know her real well under the name of Beatrice, but kept changing her name from adolescence onwards every time she changed diets, whinnied like a horse to Matua Jobey about her unhappy marriage. "Why didn't you stop me Matua?" she snorted. Riana collapsed into Matua Jobey's arms. Her husband Kelvin stared at his shoes, Matua Jobey stared out the window of the lounge, past Riana's sobbing shoulders, to the children. Four-year-old Chappy was throwing stones at cars passing by the house. Three-year-old Tinika, whose nose ran like a continuous lava flow, was trying to cross the road. With no adult in spitting distance. And twenty-month-old Manu was trying to bodyslam Miro the Rottweiler to the ground.

Matua Jobey wiped Riana's eyes. He gathered up the newspaper on the coffee table and rolled it into a baton and unceremoniously whacked his grandniece over the head.

"Whaddya on about eh?" said Matua Jobey. He never raised his voice to anyone. But the tone always rang with a little more quiet intensity when he was angry. "You have a loving and devoted husband. Three children who need parents. A huge house and two cars. And you're whining to me about not getting enough time to go down the line to the Casino? Geez you're rare Girl."

I guess there are just some things in life that, if not dealt to adequately, kinda breached Matua Jobey's personal tolerance level. Or just exasperated him. Either way, whenever that happened Matua Jobey never short-changed anyone on truth.

"You need to get out with your kids. Take them to Kohanga Reo and stay there," Matua Jobey wagged his finger at a whimpering Riana. "You might learn something Girl. Like learn to korero Te Reo ki nga tamariki." Matua Jobey turned to Kelvin. "And you." He liked him well enough. Just wished he would use his head. "Use your common sense. Get out there and teach your kids not to walk on the road. What are you? Man or mouse?"

But Matua Jobey's words were always tinged with care and concern. He never stayed angry for long. "Most of all awhi yourselves," entreated Matua Jobey to the couple, clutching their hands and holding them tight. "Then perhaps you will value a little more, the wonders of the world we live in."

That may explain why Matua Jobey was so hard on Taniora when he separated from Karli. Matua Jobey loved his son. That's why he made Taniora paint his house, car and garden shed the day Taniora went over to tell him about the separation.

"Boy, you're a fool." That was all Matua Jobey said. And he handed Taniora the paint brush and walked out the door and over to the house to Karli and the kids, before his wayward son could say anything. When he got back he found Taniora sitting on the front step. The house and car and garden shed were all newly colour co-ordinated in green and red. "Geez," thought Matua Jobey. "Looks like a flippin' circus." He looked sadly at his son. "Then again his mind must be doing flips on a trapeze."

Taniora and Matua Jobey didn't talk much after that. I tried to reconcile the two. But they were too much alike. When it came to stubbornness these two reigned supreme. With no quarter given. Nothing remotely resembling yin and yang existed here.

"I can't make him understand when he won't listen Seoul," said Taniora as he strangled his feet in the laces of his running shoes. He yanked the strings so tight that when he stood up to walk he hobbled left and right looking like a rugby player doing the ballet. Which ain't a pretty sight.

Taniora sighed long and deep. My uncle who was three years older than me looked ready to fall asleep on a train track. The level of expectation, of having his shadow overshadowed by his father had taken its toll. Maybe that's why he rushed into marriage at sixteen. He was trying to grab some sunlight of his own. "Sometimes you just have to let go and move on to better things,"

Taniora muttered to no one.

Taniora loved running. He could run for miles. He'd been doing it since he was a kid. I always had the feeling that if he could, he would run forever. That's why when me and Matua Jobey went to identify Taniora's body I made sure that my granduncle never got the chance to step onto Remuera Settlement Road. Bits and pieces of Taniora were scattered everywhere. Blue and red police and ambulance lights illuminated the fading orange skies. Putahi Mountain was straddled between day and night, its presence more felt than seen. It created an immensity so vast, comprehension was nowhere to be found. Hot luminescent pink circles were sprayed onto the black tarseal of Remuera Settlement Road.

I walked with a policeman to each circle. They glowed in the dark, revealing pieces of Taniora. With infinite care I carefully picked up each small body part and placed them in a green plastic bag. I stood over Taniora's torso, bent down and pressed my forehead and nose to his. Let the tears slowly seep into his bloodied face. I folded the flap to the plastic bag in half and gently placed it on Taniora's chest and sealed the body bag with the velcro flaps. I farewelled Taniora in my mind, turned and walked to the side of the road.

I found Matua Jobey turned towards Putahi, his mind in the cave. Talking to our ancestors. Telling them to welcome their son. I wrapped my arms around Matua Jobey and held him tight until he was ready to let go.

Taniora's tangi is a blur. Faded black and white memories of a wet and muddy Kotahitanga Marae courtyard. Bits and pieces. Lots of crying and waiata in sharp angled technicolour. Some laughter and karakia too. A long line of people across time and space, maturity and infancy, gender and class, walking into the Whare Tupuna to lay the leafy green taua at the foot of Taniora's coffin. To hongi with the living and the dead. To unravel the umbilical cord connecting Matua Jobey to us. To cut him some slack. Yet still hold on firmly as he allowed his spirit to walk a little with Taniora. Before letting him go.

But also aware of the overarching sense of infinite sadness. Where want and need suspend and combine into a slurry of tragedy. Of human potential unrealised.

Three days later, on a Sunday before lunch, we carried Taniora on the backs of waiata sung by our family to our urupa just outside Kaikohe. Taniora was not allowed to be buried on Putahi Mountain. Matua Jobey did not want Taniora to be touched by the mana that tormented him in this world. The same power that drew him to run with shadows instead of rejoicing in the sun. Matua Jobey wanted Taniora buried near his mother. He lies opposite Auntie Raina, a lone fresh grave to mark a new line for future resting places of our family.

Not long after, Matua Jobey presented me with his Scrabble board. "I don't need it anymore Boy," smiled Matua Jobey. "I'm on my way. From misery to happiness today."

Lately Matua Jobey had been tuning into "Easy Listening Taringawha 99.3 FM" with DeeJay Kaiako Raggedymouth, the only Maori Radio Deejay to play Scottish music.

Hence Matua Jobey's kiaoracation to the Proclaimers.

"So what are you gonna do instead of making words?" I asked.

Matua Jobey patted me on the back. "I'm gonna make sentences Boy." And that's what he did. He grabbed his father's old books. The ones with all the history of our family. And he wrote stories about us. About all sixty-two generations who have been here since our ancestor Kupe surfskied into Hokianga Harbour and left a couple of taniwha in the Harbour entrance to stop anyone gaining access to his pad.

Matua Jobey still writes today. He's working on a set of poems for Taniora. "Just my way of talking to him you know Boy?" smiled Matua Jobey when he told me. "My pen is my telephone to him now."

Matua Jobey even got published you know. A book about poor jazz musicians. It's called *The Manuka Trees Are Crying*. It was a bestseller. Well, Uncle Tane bought two hundred and fifty copies and sent them to his grandchildren in Australia. Porangi Thomas bought a hundred copies too. He sells them in his boutique butcher shop in Auckland. Children of Irish migrants buy a copy with half a dozen Snarler Classics.

The Teina brothers and their work crew have finished cleaning the Waitangi River. It looks real good. Rawiri Teina has set up a carving school on the right side of the river. He gets master carvers from down the line to come in and help revive the discipline amongst our own.

On the left side of the river, Karli and Auntie Kataraina have started a school too. They teach young women how to make korowai. But they do more than that. They teach people how to laugh and cry when those they love refuse to love them back. Not to bottle the anxiety and worry up inside. Karli has decided to stay here now. Rawiri is helping her deal with the hurt. By telling her it's all right to let go of the pain.

I live in Auckland city now. But even though it's a three hour drive away, I'm still a regular at Matua Jobey's place. Every Christmas I hitch up from Auckland. I usually get dropped off at the bottom of Waiwera Road. That's okay though. I don't mind. Because I get to stand still just outside Matua Jobey's gate, at the foot of Putahi Mountain. I can see Matua Jobey sitting at his desk, in front of his new computer, slowly tapping out new sentences to old ideas. I pause for a moment. Drink the picture in. I fumble for the velcro on my backpack. With infinite care I open the backpack. Pull out my copy of *The Manuka Trees Are Crying*. And I walk up the footpath to the house to greet my Kaumatua.

Contributors

Kateri Akiwenzie-Damm is an Anishnaabe writer of mixed descent from the Chippewas of Nawash First Nation on the Saugeen Peninsula in south western Ontario. In 1993 Kateri was coordinator of "Beyond Survival" an International Indigenous Writers, Visual and Performing Arts Conference and in 1998 she organized "To See Proudly: Advancing Indigenous Arts Beyond the Millennium" a national First Peoples arts conference. Her writing has been published in anthologies, journals, and magazines in North America, Aotearoa, Australia, and Germany. A collection of her poetry *my heart is a stray bullet* was published in 1993. *bloodriver woman*, a poetry chapbook was published by absinthe chapbooks in 1998. Readings of her work have been broadcast nationally in Canada on WTN. Spoken word pieces of her poetry have been distributed on various audio cassette compilations and broadcast nationally on CBC radio. Kateri is currently working on a CD of spoken word poetry with a group of international Indigenous musicians and friends.

Sherman Alexie is a Spokane/Coeur d'Alene writer from the Spokane Indian Reservation. He is the award-winning author of several books of poetry, a collection of short stories, *The Lone Ranger and Tonto Fistfight in Heaven*, and two novels, *Reservation Blues*, and his most recent, *Indian Killer*. *The Business of Fancydancing*, his critically acclaimed first collection of poetry and prose, was selected as a *New York Times Book Review* Notable Book of the Year in 1992. It was followed by *I Would Steal Horses*, the winner of Slipstream's Fifth Annual Chapbook Contest, *Old Shirts & New Skins*, and *First Indian on the Moon*. *Smoke Signals*, a feature movie based on an original script by Sherman, was released in 1998 and was a winner at the Sundance Film Festival.

Kimberly Blaeser is an enrolled member of the Minnesota Chippewa Tribe, and grew up on the White Earth Reservation in Northwestern Minnesota. Currently an Associate Professor of English at the University of Wisconsin–Milwaukee, she teaches courses in Native American Literature, Creative Writing, and American Nature Writing. She lives with her husband, son, and daughter in rural Wisconsin. Her books include a critical study of Anishnaabe writer Gerald Vizenor, and a collection of poetry that won the 1993 First Book Award from the Native Writers' Circle of the Americas. Her poetry, short fiction, personal essays, and scholarly articles have been widely anthologized in Canada and the United States.

Joseph Bruchac lives with his wife, Carol, in the Adirondack mountain foothills town of Greenfield Center, New York where he was raised. Much of his writing draws on that region and his Abenaki ancestry — part of an ethnic background that includes Slovak and English blood. He, his younger sister Margaret, and his two grown sons, James and Jesse, have worked extensively in the preservation of Abenaki language and culture. His honours include a Rockefeller Humanities fellowship, an NEA Poetry fellowship, and the Lifetime Achievement Award from the Native Writers Circle of the Americas. His poems, articles and stories have appeared in over 500 publications, from *American Poetry Review* to *National Geographic* and he has edited such highly praised anthologies as *Songs from this Earth on Turtle's Back* and *Returning the Gift*. His most recent books include *Sacajawea*, a novel, *Squanto's Journey*, a picture book, and *No Borders*, a collection of poems.

Maria Campbell is a Metis author, film maker, teacher, and activist, born in north west Saskatchewan and raised in a traditional Metis trapping lifestyle. Her first book, *Halfbreed*, was published in 1973 and is a classic in Aboriginal literature. Maria has also published *Riel's People, People of the Buffalo, Achimoona, The Book of Jessica*, and *Stories of the Road Allowance People*. "Dah Teef" first appeared in *Stories of the Road Allowance People*, published in 1995 by Theytus Books. A recipient of an Aboriginal Achievement Award for her work, Maria is one of the most respected and important Indigenous writers in Canada.

Josie Douglas is of Wardaman descent: her grandmother's country is just south of Katherine in Australia's Northern Territory. Josie has worked in the publishing industry for seven years, and has spoken throughout Australia on Indigenous literature and publishing. She commissioned the anthology *Message Stick: Contemporary Aboriginal Writing* for IAD Press and has worked on a wide range of fiction, trade and academic titles. She has a Bachelor of Arts (Australian Studies) from the University of South Australia and currently lives in Alice Springs with her partner and children.

Louise Erdrich was born in Little Falls, Minnesota, on June 7, 1954. The daughter of a French Ojibwe mother and German American father, Louise Erdrich is a member of the Turtle Mountain Band of Chippewa. She is the author of several novels including *Love Medicine, The Beet Queen, Tracks, The Bingo Palace*, and *Tales of Burning Love*. Her latest novel is *The Antelope's Wife*. Louise has received numerous awards and prizes including the 1975 Academy of American Poets Prize, the Best Fiction Award from the American Academy and Institute of Arts and Letters, the Sue Kaufman Prize for Best First Fiction from the American Academy of Arts and Letters, the National Book Critics Circle award for the year's best novelist, and the American Book Award from the Before Columbus Foundation. Louise has published several books of poetry including *Imagination* (1981), *Jacklight* (1984) and *Baptism of Desire* (1989). She has also published a book of non-fiction titled *The Blue Jay's Dance*.

Richard Frankland was born in 1963 and is of Gunditjmara descent. He is an award-winning writer and director of short films, most notably *Harry's War* and *No Way to Forget*. In 1996 *No Way to Forget* was invited to be screened at the 49th Cannes International Film Festival. The film also won two Australian Film Institute (AFI) awards including Best Short Film, the first film by an Indigenous director to win an AFI award.

In March 2000, *Harry's War* won the Hollywood Black Film Festival Jury Prize at the Film Festival Prize in Hollywood. As well as making a name as one of Australia's leading independent film makers, Richard is a talented musician, songwriter, theatre director and writer.

Patricia Grace was born in Wellington, Aotearoa in 1937. She is of Ngati Raukawa, Ngati Toa, and Te Ati Awa descent, and is affiliated to Ngati Porou by marriage. She has five collections of short stories, four children's books, four novels and she wrote the text for *Wahine Toa: Women of Maori Myth*, illustrated by artist Robyn Kahukiwa. Her first book, *Waiariki*, published in 1975, was the first collection of stories by a Maori woman writer. Patricia's stories have been published in numerous periodicals and anthologies internationally. She has won many awards including the Children's Picture Book of the Year award, and the New Zealand Book Award for fiction. Her fourth novel *Baby No Eyes* was released by Penguin in September 1998. She has recently completed her fifth novel.

Briar Grace-Smith is an award winning writer of plays and her fiction has been anthologized in various anthologies and journals. She has won three national playwrighting awards including the Tripp-Chapman award, Absolutely Positively Outstanding New New Zealand Play award, and the Bruce Mason Playwrights Award. Briar is of Ngapuhi ancestry and lives in Paekakariki, on the North Island of Aotearoa, with musician Himiona Grace and their three children. Briar was the Writer in Residence at Massey University and recently completed a collection of short stories, *Wearing Tangaroa's Eyebrows*. Her play *Purapurawhetu* has been praised as "a new classic" and received the Absolutely Positively Outstanding New New Zealand Play award in 1997. Briar is an avid weaver and has been studying Maori language at "Te Wananga O Raukawa." Her award-winning play *Purapurawhetu* recently toured Canada and Greece.

Linda Hogan is a Chickasaw writer whose published works include poetry, fiction and non-fiction. Among her published books are two volumes of poetry: *The Book of Medicines*, and *Seeing through the Sun*, which received an American Book Award. Her non-fiction includes *Dwellings: A Spiritual History of the Living World* published by Touchstone. She has published three novels, the Pulitzer Prize finalist *Mean Spirit*, *Solar Storms* and her most recent novel, *Power*. Linda has received the Oklahoma Book Award, the Colorado Book Award, the Mountains and Plains Booksellers Award, a Guggenheim Fellowship, a National Endowment for the Arts and a Lannan Foundation award. She teaches at the University of Colorado in Boulder.

Witi Ihimaera is descended from Te Aitanga A Mahaki, Rongowhakaata and Ngati Porou with close affiliations to Tuhoe, Te Whanau A Apanui, Kahungunu, and Ngai Tamanuhiri. His award-winning works include the novel *The Matriarch*, which won the Wattie Book of the Year Award, *Tangi* (winner of the Wattie Award), and *Bulibasha, King of the Gypsies* (winner of the Montana Book of the Year Award in 1995). Other works include *Pounamu, Pounamu*, *The Whale Rider*, *Dear Miss Mansfield*, *Nights in the Garden of Spain*, and *The New Net Goes Fishing*. Witi is also a playwright. His first play *Woman Far Walking*, debuted at the New Zealand Festival of the Arts in Wellington in March 2000.

Witi now lives in Auckland and lectures in the English department at Auckland University, specializing in New Zealand literature and creative writing.

Alootook Ipellie is an Inuk writer who was born in a camp near Iqaluit, Northwest Territories, where he spent his childhood and adolescence. In 1973 he moved to Ottawa to study and pursue a career in art. Alootook is an important figure in the Inuit literature movement. The former editor of "Inuit Today," and "Inuit," his writing and artwork first appeared in the anthology of Inuit writing *Paper Stays Put*, published in 1978. Since then his work has been published in various journals and anthologies. His book *Arctic Dreams and Nightmares*, published by Theytus Books, contains interconnected short stories with accompanying pen ink drawings. "Love Triangle" first appeared in *Arctic Dreams and Nightmares*, one of the few books in Canada written by an Inuk writer.

Thomas King is of Cherokee, German and Greek descent. His work includes two novels: *Medicine River*, which was subsequently made into a movie for CBC-TV, and the highly praised *Green Grass, Running Water*. His collection of short stories, *One Good Story, That One*, was published in 1993. His children's book *A Coyote Columbus Story* was nominated for a Governor General's award.

Zion A. Komene was born and raised in Pewhairangi, or what is more commonly known as the Bay of Islands in the Far North of the North Island of Aotearoa–New Zealand. He draws his whakapapa genealogy from the Ngati Rehia and Ngai Ta Wake hapu of his father's family, which sits well alongside the Ngati Rahiri and Te Uri O Hua hapu of his mother's people. All of these hapu are part of the greater hapu of Ngapuhi nui tonu. Zion was educated at the home of his Kaumatua (elder), Kahi Waikerepuru Rameka, next door to the pyramid that held the annual kumara harvest, and at the University of Auckland. He lives in Auckland city. He is currently completing his first major work, *The Kahurangi Garden*, a collection of short stories.

Kenny Laughton was born in 1950 and has tribal affiliations with the Eastern Arrernte people of Central Australia. He joined the army in 1968 and served in Vietnam, returning to Central Australia on his discharge in 1971. Between 1991 and 1996 he served successively as director of a number of Aboriginal organisations in Alice Springs, despite the gradual deterioration of his health due to war-related illnesses and injuries. Late in 1996 he was assessed as TPI (Totally and Permanently Incapacitated) and awarded a pension by the Department of Veterans' Affairs. Since his enforced retirement, Kenny has been writing. Co-author of *The Aboriginal Ex-servicemen of Central Australia*, he ventured towards fiction — or faction — for the first time with *Not Quite Men, no longer boys*. He is currently working on *Finders Keepers*, an epic novel based in the Central Australian goldfields.

Melissa Lucashenko, born in 1967, is a Murri woman of mixed European and Yugambeh/Bundjalung descent, and has affiliations with the Arrernte and Waanyi peoples. Melissa worked in blue collar jobs including martial arts instruction and bar work before attending Griffith University, where she received an Honours degree in politics. Her first novel, *Steam Pigs*, won the 1998 Dobbie Award for Australian women's fiction and was shortlisted for the NSW Premier's Literary Award. *Killing Darcy*, a young adult novel, won the Royal Blind Society Award for Young Adult Talking Books in 1999. Melissa's third book is an adult novel concerning Indigenous deaths in custody and stolen generations issues and will soon be released.

Sally Morgan was born in Perth, Western Australia and is of Palyku descent. *My Place* was her first book, and upon publication it immediately achieved best-seller status. Sally is also an established children's author and artist. She has works in numerous private collections and in national galleries throughout Australia. Sally is currently the Director at The Centre for Indigenous History and the Arts at the University of Western Australia.

Bruce Pascoe was born in Richmond, Victoria (Australia) in 1947. He graduated as a secondary teacher but has also worked as a farmer, fisherman and barman. He now runs Pascoe Publishing with his wife, Lyn. Until recently, they also published the successful quarterly *Australian Short Stories*. He has two children and lives at Cape Otway in Victoria, where he is a proud member of the Wathaurong Aboriginal Cooperative. His books include *Night Animals* (stories, 1986) and three novels: *Fox* (1988), *Ruby-eyed Coucal* (1996) and *Shark* (1999).

Richard Van Camp is a member of the Dogrib Nation from the Northwest Territories in Canada. He is the proud husband of Michelle Reid of the Heiltsuk Nation. "Mermaids" was originally commissioned by CBC Radio as a radio drama for their 1999 Festival of Fiction where it was narrated by Cree actor, Ben Cardinal, and was broadcast nationally several times. Richard is the author of a novel, *The Lesser Blessed*, and two children's books: *A Man Called Raven* and *What's The Most Beautiful Thing You Know About Horses?* with Cree artist George Littlechild as the illustrator. Richard and Michelle currently live in Bella Bella, British Columbia, with their dog Chuckles.

Alexis Wright is a member of the Waanyi people from the highlands of the southern Gulf of Carpentaria. She has worked extensively for many Aboriginal organisations as a writer, researcher and educator in the areas of Indigenous land and culture issues. She now lives in Alice Springs. Her previous publications include: *Plains of Promise*, *Grog War*, and *Take Power, like this old man here* (ed.). Her novel *Plains of Promise* was shortlisted in the Commonwealth Writers' Prize — first book category, the *Age* Book of the Year and the NSW Premier's Awards. Alexis is also a widely published short story writer and the short story *When Devils Call* won the Northern Territory Aboriginal and Torres Strait Islander Writers' Award in 1994. Alexis is currently the recipient of a two-year Writing Fellowship from the Aboriginal and Torres Strait Islander Board of the Australia Council and is working on her next novel.